MISADVENTURES

OF A

CITY GIRL

BY
MEREDITH WILD & CHELLE BLISS

MISADVENTURES

OF A

CITY GIRL

BY
MEREDITH WILD & CHELLE BLISS

WATERHOUSE PRESS

To my mother, we've been through hell and back, but there's no one else I'd rather have by my side.
- Chelle

Chelle, this one is for you. For your fierce love, incredible strength, and unfailing friendship... I'm forever grateful.
- Meredith

CHAPTER ONE

MADISON

Pop!

My heart leaps at the sound. A rush of fizz pours from the top of the champagne bottle, dousing my hands. I curse inwardly and mop the mess off the counter. Not bothering with a glass, I take the bottle with me to the couch and curl up for another quiet night in. I flip through the channels and settle on a made-for-TV movie. All I need is a pint of Ben & Jerry's to complete my look as a miserable divorcée.

I thought when all the paperwork was finalized today, something would change... *I* would change. I was no longer Madison Cleary, the wife on the arm of a rising star. I was officially Madison Atwood again. The new Madison should feel happy and relieved and free. But something about this celebration feels so incredibly empty.

I close my eyes and exhale a tired sigh.

Goddamn him. As hard as I try, I can't seem to let go of my anger.

Rejection. Hope. Failure. Determination. Yes...determination is here and fighting for ground too.

I put the bottle down and reach for my laptop. The Internet

has answers and surely this isn't the end for me. The failure of my marriage has been a devastating blow, without a doubt. But I can't let my famous and infamously unfaithful husband—*ex-husband*—jeopardize my future.

Sometimes it feels like he's everywhere, though. Clients, gigs, and friends still exist in our shared circles. If I ever want to feel completely myself again, I need a break. I need to get away from LA, the whispers, and the chapter of my life that I'd just signed into the past.

A trip to Baja, maybe. Meet a sexy, rich producer who would blacklist the fucker I'd stood by so faithfully through his rise to fame. We'd sip expensive champagne and eat just enough decadent food to fuel our back-to-back sexcapades. And of course we'd kill time in between by frolicking in the clear blue ocean.

I let that fantasy play out for a few minutes before tugging my thoughts back to reality, or at least a more realistic getaway. The last few months of marriage to Jeremy and the subsequent months negotiating our divorce had produced the most anguished dry spell I had experienced since high school. Jeremy and I had met as naïve, fumbling teenagers. We'd been together ever since. I'd been stupid in love with him then.

The memory hits me, but the pain hits me harder—deep in my gut, before it travels up my esophagus causing a painful burn. Goddamn. All those memories are tainted now, and I hate him for that more than anything.

Maybe it won't always be this way. Maybe one day I'll heal. He'll be a memory, but a distant one. I won't always feel this way...

Emotionally charged, I start a new search for spa retreats. As much as I wish I could fuck the feelings away on a tropical island with a beautiful stranger, I know no good will come from that. I need a real break. Something restorative. Something that can heal all the tears in my heart.

The first few search results return locations in northern California. Far enough from LA, but close enough that I could come back for work in a pinch. I click through website after website. The options are either too dated, too crunchy, or tout a brand of spirituality I'm not ready for. I don't want to be converted. I just need some quiet time, maybe a few massages, and some fresh mountain air.

Pure determination brings me to the second page of results. I click on the website for Avalon Springs Retreat. My heart lifts and brings some hope up with it. Avalon Springs is basically a spa in the mountains. Home-cooked meals, yoga classes, a few outdoor excursions, and big blocks of time meant to help people re-center. The owners look like legit hippies. The accommodations appear clean and comfortable. And it doesn't seem like a convoluted tourist trap for the prima donnas I'm hoping to take a break from.

I check my schedule, ignore the pricing—because I deserve this no matter the cost—and book a four-week stay.

Today I am Madison Atwood, and the next chapter of my life is going to start at Avalon Springs.

◆ ◆ ◆ ◆

"Here's your room key. You have a king suite in the Olive Annex, which is that way. It's only the next building over, so you're not far from the dining room and the classes." The young girl with flawless skin and thick blond dreads points to the front entrance of the retreat. "Every Saturday we do an orientation session here in the main house. That'll start in about an hour."

"An orientation?" I lift my gaze from the paper nametag where *Indigo* is written in sloppy script to her pale gray eyes.

She smiles loosely, as if she hasn't experienced an ounce of tension in her life. "Yeah. It's kind of like a meet and greet. You'll introduce yourself to the other residents, do some breathing exercises and stretching, and Vi and Lou will talk a little bit more about the springs."

"Great," I mutter, not bothering to disguise my lack of enthusiasm. I doubt this easy-breezy flower child will pick up on it anyway.

I tuck the cool metal key into my back pocket, a small sign of my commitment to this getaway that I already fear is a complete and utter mistake. The reception area is noisy as a pack of people linger outside what appears to be a yoga class. Or maybe it's the beginning of the orientation gathering. Anxiety hits and the familiar burn in my stomach follows.

There is nothing quiet about this. Nothing restorative. Sure, this is a definite break from the city scene, but these are *not my people.* I can rub shoulders with Hollywood's rich and famous, but five minutes with this enlightened collective is sending me into a tailspin.

I cut Indigo off before she can finish her intro speech, grab the check-in paperwork, and head out the front door a lot faster than I came through it. The journey from my Beamer to my room is mercifully short, although I'm not thrilled to be staying so close to the epicenter of this "quiet mountainside retreat."

I send up a tiny prayer of thanks that at least the room delivers. It's all as advertised—clean, cozy, and spacious. After a quick tour of the room's amenities, I peek out the window to see what or who is making the noise. A stream of apparently eager "residents" are filing into the main building. Yoga pants and head bands seem to be the uniform. I stare down at my outfit—torn jeans, a tight V-neck, and a pair of well-loved Chucks.

Decidedly out of my element, I grab my key and the map of the property that I'd all but torn out of Indigo's hand and head out. I walk briskly past the small crowd and keep moving until they are only a quiet murmur of activity behind me.

The landscape here is different than anything I'm used to. I'd been an East Coast girl all my life, always working on my career, and—once we came out west—*his* career, so I rarely made it to the more scenic places in California.

As I follow a wide, worn path that weaves into denser areas, my thoughts are loud. Doubt. Regret. Hopelessness. They shout and cling to me. If I walked into that orientation right now, I'd be wearing it all over me. I'd be a beacon of not belonging. That lost woman whose husband left her because she wasn't the quintessential arm candy he needed her to be. The rejection and the pain feel like a big, ugly tattoo that no amount of time will ever be able to wear off.

I push myself farther, vaguely noting the incline and the fine sheen of perspiration that beads on my skin as I go. Maybe Avalon Springs isn't the haven I truly need. But I've come this far...

Tears burn behind my eyes because I'm alone. So utterly alone.

Clusters of pines hug the trail. Above the treetops, the sky is a majestic shade of purple. My thoughts quiet enough for me to realize that despite being well away from the retreat center now, night is coming on and I have no idea where I am or where I'm going. But the faint sound of water lures me forward.

Beyond the trees is a clearing, a well of water at its center. Despite the cooler temperature at this elevation, steam swirls off the vibrant turquoise pool. I scale a smooth, round rock and test the temperature of the water with my fingertips. Perfect, like a freshly drawn bath.

This must be *the* Avalon Springs. The retreat's namesake promises healing properties from the mineral deposits that run off the nearby mountains. Rivulets of water trail off higher rocks and down into nature's most perfect bath tub.

After taking a quick glance around, I act. I strip my clothes and dip my naked toes into the water. Then, with care, I submerge my body. I let my head slip underwater, and my hair swirls like a thousand strands of silk around my bare shoulders. I groan with relief and bubbles float through the clear water to the surface. I take turns swimming and sinking my whole body deep into the water. The heat and the water, being unburdened of my clothes and all those heavy thoughts... Nothing has ever felt so good.

My toes find the bottom, and I launch myself back to the surface when I need air. After a while I wade to a place where I can easily stand. My breasts hover just above the surface of the water. I pull myself onto a wide, flat rock that frames the pool and lie on it, unbothered that it's both hard and cool against my skin. I'm warm and relaxed from my swim in the springs.

I close my eyes, enjoying the simple sounds of water and birds and the isolation that I'd hiked all this way to find. I skim my hands over my skin, and for the first time in what seems like forever, I notice a faint pulse between my thighs. God, I'm strung so tight lately. So in need of release. Encouraged that my body is still paying attention to some of my basic needs, I touch and tease myself to a higher point of arousal.

Getting close, I spread my thighs and dip a finger into my pussy while the other plays my clit like a record. Minutes pass as I deftly manipulate the places that ache for the attention of a man. And not just any man. One who won't break me all over again. I don't have one of those, so for now, my touch will have to do.

My breathing ticks up with my pace. I've brought myself to this point a thousand times. I know just what to do. More times than not, though, the act leaves me feeling empty. Physically satisfied, but never emotionally. I don't care. After the five-hour drive from the city, I need a release. I curve my fingers deeper into my pussy and graze the tips rhythmically across the rough pad of skin inside. The soft head of a man's engorged cock would feel better there, but whatever.

I lick my lips and imagine a man is pleasing me right now. Thick and brawny, passion in his eyes, he's filling me with every inch of his silky cock. He's telling me I'm beautiful, that I feel better than anyone he's ever had. He's grazing over that magic spot, over...and over...and...

With a sharp inhale, I bow off the rock, so close, so ready. My heels and shoulder blades press hard against the rock. I release a cry that's half arousal and half frustration, because the orgasm is just beyond reach.

I open my eyes. Stars puncture the navy sky with tiny pinpricks of light. I glance back to the trail and push down a flash of worry that I might not be able to find my way back.

Then I see him through the trees. And I scream.

LUKE

I'm not sure what possessed me to stop and watch her. She'd been loud enough marching up the path. Another city girl passing through the retreat at the base of the mountain, no doubt. I'd come here tonight to enjoy the springs because Saturday is their turnover day and the new residents rarely venture up past sunset.

But the second this woman's clothes hit the ground, I couldn't move. I should have made my way back to my cabin up the mountainside, but instead I watched her swim and float like a goddess through the water. She had long brown hair that clung in a straight slick v down her back when she rose above the water, revealing possibly the most perfect set of breasts I'd ever seen on a woman.

And then, with only a little guilt, I watched her slide up on that rock and plunge her slender fingers into her pussy until her cries echoed off the rocks and rendered the forest and my breathing silent. Now I'm hard, in absolutely no condition to comfortably return home. And I can't in good conscience leave her up here as night quickly falls around us.

When our eyes locked, she screamed and slipped back into the water to hide her nakedness. I adjust myself enough to disguise how her little display has affected me and walk closer.

"Who are you?" Her voice is shaky with panic. She stares at me wide-eyed, probably contemplating if I'm going to do her any harm.

At this hour, this far from the retreat, she is wise to worry. Nothing could protect her from someone of my size and skillset if I had malicious intentions.

"I'm not going to hurt you," I offer gently, hoping to ease her fears. "You're out here pretty late. Do you know your way back?"

She folds her arms over her chest, even though I can't see anything under the water anyway.

"I have a map."

I smirk and glance briefly at the pile of clothes she'd abandoned for the springs. "Yeah? Do you have a flashlight to read the map?"

Grooves mark the space between her dark winged brows. Her eyes are stunning in their shape and intensity, even if I couldn't place the precise color in the fading light.

"I can take you back. Someone like you shouldn't be out here alone."

Her frown deepens. "Someone like me?"

"You're at least a mile from the retreat. You have no supplies and no provisions. Someone without a healthy fear of the wild outdoors, at this hour or any other, shouldn't be out here alone."

"I don't need rescuing, okay?"

I resist the urge to roll my eyes. Another asshole from the city with too much ego and not enough sense. "Let's go. I'll take you back."

Slowly she moves to the edge toward her clothes, never taking her eyes off me. "Look away, please."

I laugh. "I've seen a lot more than you're about to show me."

Her eyes widened and her nostrils flare. Without another word, I turn casually to give her privacy that seems pointless after what I just witnessed. A minute later, the sound of her sneakers scraping against the rock prompts me to turn. She is fully dressed, and I allow myself a moment to appreciate her body with clothes on. Her jeans hug her thighs nicely, and her breasts look fuller in the tight shirt.

I dislodge the thoughts around that assessment before my cock starts misbehaving again. I haven't been with a woman in a long time, and even though I despise everything this one probably stands for, I can't help that the beast in me wants to tear her clothes off and bury myself inside her until we both come. Repeatedly.

I mutter a curse under my breath before turning and heading swiftly down the path.

A few minutes pass and I don't need to look back. I hear ragged breathing and branches cracking under her careful footing—signs she is struggling to keep up. She has no business in the woods. Why Lou and Vi keep luring these idiots to this beautiful place is beyond me. People like her will never belong here. They'll never appreciate this place the way they should. A week in the mountains is a fashion statement for most of these people, and I just want them out of my woods and off my mountain so I can enjoy what I came here for. Solitude. Peace. A simple life. A quiet dip in the springs without some sexy little city girl cluttering up my thoughts with her sweet pussy...because I'm pretty sure it's sweet, and oh so tight.

I halt in my tracks and spin. The brunette nearly barrels into me. I catch her by the shoulders when she tips off balance. Somehow she feels smaller in my arms, just a little bit of flesh covering the delicate structure of her frame. Her wet hair dampens her shirt, drawing my attention to that lovely rack again. Goddamn, this woman is a distraction I didn't ask for.

"You can get there from here," I say gruffly.

Her eyes go wide again. "I can?"

The moonlight glints on her skin. If she'd worn makeup, the springs had washed it away, leaving her natural and bare. She's definitely pretty. A pert nose and a little bow of a mouth. There's nothing exotic or stark about her features, but she's someone who looks perfectly gorgeous with no effort.

I release my hold on her and jab my thumb in the direction behind me. "It's just a few yards down the path. You'll see the lights, and they will lead you the rest of the way."

"Thank you," she says softly, almost too softly to hear if not for the near silence of the woods at night. Gone is the tone she'd given me earlier. How she'd gone from rapture to claiming that she didn't need rescuing, I didn't know. But maybe that had been fear talking.

I wince, because I don't like the idea of being feared. I'd never hurt her, or anyone. Even if I didn't want them in my woods. "You don't have to thank me."

"Yes, I do. You could have left me there, or..."

"Or?" I lift an eyebrow, challenging her to say it out loud.

True enough, I could have done all the things I couldn't stop thinking about right now. I could have gotten myself between her silky thighs, plunged into her, stretched her pussy around me, and satisfied her in ways those pretty little fingers never would.

But she doesn't say any of that. She doesn't say a word. She only gazes up at me, and for a second I wonder if she can read my thoughts, if somehow this unexpected depravity radiates off me. Then her hands slide up the front of my chest, and I almost forget how to breathe.

"What's your name?" Her voice is a whisper now, like she's hiding from her own words.

When had a woman touched me last? I can't fucking breathe.

"Good night."

I push past her, forcing my legs to move me back up the trail. I have to get the hell away from her.

CHAPTER TWO

MADISON

What the hell was that? I asked him a simple question and he stalked off like a savage without so much as a response. He dismissed me like I was the one who'd intruded on his private moment, not the other way around.

Fueled by anger, I make my way down the trail toward the main house, following the light just as he told me. My legs ache, the strain from the hike making each step feel like it may be my last.

Leaning forward, I rest my hands on my knees, giving myself a moment to catch my breath. All I can think about is him—the sexy stranger who came out of nowhere and, although he'd watched me, hadn't wanted to engage.

The lights from the expansive windows spanning the back of the lodge illuminate the clearing only a dozen yards in front of me. Pushing off my knees, I propel myself forward to the only place I want to be—my room.

I take a few steps and the memory of touching him stops me. *Oh God.* I touched him too. Why did I do that? Maybe I misread the look in his eyes before I slid my hand up the front of his chest. The hard muscles underneath my palm felt like steel. He brushed past me and disappeared like I'd offended him in some way.

As I break through the brush and reach the clearing, I see Indigo standing on the wraparound wooden deck, staring off into space.

When she spots me, she waves frantically. "Oh my God, Ms. Atwood! We were looking for you."

I climb the steps slowly and hold onto the railing to keep my balance. "I didn't mean to be gone so long."

"I almost sent out the search party when you weren't in your room and didn't show up at orientation."

"Sorry." I'm not being sincere. The last thing I wanted to do tonight was go to an orientation. I came here to be alone and get away from it all. Not be surrounded by strangers and follow a schedule.

"It's okay. I made you an appointment with Vi tomorrow." She smiles brightly, coming to my side when I finally make it to the main level. "She's going to give you a private tour of the property. It's very important to us that our guests have the best experience possible."

"Uh, thanks." My lack of enthusiasm is evident in my voice, but when her smile fades I try to recover. "I appreciate you looking after me, Indigo."

She places her hand on my arm and gives it a light squeeze. "We're only trying to help."

"I know. It's just been a long day."

"Well," she says filled with excitement, "I can make you a nice cup of cocoa to help you relax."

"No." My refusal comes a little too fast, but I've hit my limit of happy people for today. "I just need a bath and some sleep. I appreciate the offer though. It's very kind of you."

"All part of the job. If you change your mind, we're going to be having a campfire starting around nine down there." She motions to the right side of the clearing where a man is throwing logs into a pit and another is rearranging chairs in a circle. "Stop by maybe. It always helps me sleep."

I have a feeling that nothing has kept her up a night in her life. There's a lightness to Indigo that I wish I could feel again. Something I'm sure I had in my youth, before reality slapped me in the face. "Night, Indigo." I smile softly.

"Night, Ms. Atwood. Sleep tight."

Restful sleep has eluded me since news of Jeremy's infidelity graced every gossip rag in town. Some of the more serious news outlets even picked up the story, making the affair inescapable. The incessant phone calls and text messages had kept me awake and unable to move on from the heartbreak with the constant reminder of how I'd been wronged.

After I make my way to my room and take a shower, I crawl under the covers and stare up at the ceiling. No matter how hard I try, sleep escapes me. The only thing I can think about is the mysterious man in the woods. The asshole who brushed me off. The one I wanted to touch again. What would his bare chest feel like against my palms?

"Fuck." I hiss and slam my hands against the mattress.

I should be pissed at him for watching me, but remembering the look in his eyes when I caught him turns me on. No one has looked at me like that in ages. Living in LA does little for a woman's ego. Girls barely out of high school are all the rage and everyone else is getting plastic surgery to look more youthful than they really are.

But he looked at me with pure lust, the same way Jeremy did

before he strayed. The mystery man may have stalked off, but I know that he wanted me in that moment. Feeling the familiar, dull ache between my legs, I reach under the covers and touch myself. My eyes seal shut and images of the handsome, mysterious man flood my mind.

Something about his beauty... His eyes were hooded and rivaled the darkest night sky. Though his eyes were striking, his hair surprised me the most. The dirty blond streaks in his long wild hair matched the honey, tanned skin on his face. Even pulled back into a messy man bun, the look worked for him. His beard, something I'd never found attractive on a man, made his features more pronounced and impossibly more manly.

Picking up where I left off in the springs, I pretend instead of my own fingers, he is pounding into me. There's hunger in his eyes as he moans my name. He glides his rugged hands across my skin, scorching my flesh in their wake. I dig my heels into his ass, feeling the clench of his muscles with each pump. I'm unable to control my voice, my moans growing louder with each stroke.

The orgasm that eluded me earlier hits me hard now. I cry out, working my fingers in and out while rubbing my palm against my clit. My muscles tense as the waves of pleasure crash over me repeatedly and my body twists to one side. When the final crest crashes down, my eyes fly open and I gasp for air.

"Huh," I mutter on an exhale, still trying to catch my breath. Never in my life have I come so quickly. Not even after Jeremy spent so much time working me up that I couldn't even see straight. Even then, it took me at least ten minutes to reach an orgasm that was anything close to earth shattering. But this one, thinking of *him,* rocked my fucking world.

I'm too exhausted to overanalyze the situation. Closing my eyes, I try to clear my mind and focus on the crickets chirping outside my window. But it's no use. All I see is him.

LUKE

The last thing I expected last night was a naked woman, alone, pleasuring herself at the springs. Orientation day at Avalon should've been my time to enjoy that slice of the property without worry.

My grandfather left me the land—over fifty acres of pristine, secluded mountaintop in Northern California. I never planned to make it my home. The site sat abandoned for years with the cabin falling into disrepair. But when my last tour of duty ended, the thought of going back to my old life and being part of civilian society sent me into a tailspin.

Instead, I put my blood, sweat, and tears into this place and made it my home.

This was supposed to be my escape.

My haven from the outside world.

Until *she* showed up.

I sit and stare into the fire while I sip my morning coffee. I can't stop picturing the way her chestnut hair, dampened and wild, clung to her clothing, outlining her breasts. Her perfect breasts. Her perky breasts. Her plump breasts. *Think about something else, dumbass.* The last time I touched a pair was... Hell, it's been years.

Before joining the Navy, I'd had dreams of a normal life. None of them involved living in the woods, high up on a mountain, alone. I always thought I'd have the American dream—get married, buy a house, and fill it with so many kids I'd eventually end up driving a shitty minivan.

But my time in the military fucked that up. I thought I was prepared for whatever I was going to experience during my enlistment. I'd seen and done things I didn't want to relive or repeat, but I didn't have any issues coping until my last tour of duty. There didn't seem to be any rhyme or reason to our assignments. The violence seemed senseless.

By the time I was discharged as a decorated Navy SEAL, I couldn't imagine going back to "normal" life. My PTSD was so severe that even the sound of a car backfiring set me off. The only cure was self-imposed isolation.

I can function around people if I need to. Every now and again I venture into town but never stay long. I know the way everyone else lives, but that's not my world anymore. I'm better off alone. I prefer the peacefulness of my mountain.

Typically, my daily chores keep me occupied enough that my mind doesn't wander. But today all I can think of is the brown-haired beauty with her soft moans and killer tits. I should've left as soon as I laid eyes on her, but something about the way the moon glistened off her damp skin kept me glued to the spot. When she cried out, I lost all ability to think straight.

When she saw me, there was nothing but fear in her eyes. I'd seen that look a million times when I served in the military. I couldn't take the weight of it again. I couldn't leave without easing her mind and trying to satisfy my own conscience. I would never hurt her. Violence wasn't my style or in my nature. I'd sworn to serve and protect, not attack and scare.

But...I couldn't deny wanting to lean forward and press my body against hers... Plunge my tongue deep into her mouth. When she touched me, I'd wanted to act upon the fantasy, but then reality set in.

How could she be so frightened one minute and touching me the next? She had looked like she wanted me to kiss her... Of course I did the only thing that felt right—I ran.

The contact had shocked me.

Completely rocked me to my core.

Like a fucking asshole I turned my back on her, leaving her to fend for herself. I shouldn't have left her, but I didn't ask for company. *Fuck.* If she didn't make it back, Vi, Lou, and an entire search party would be canvassing the area, looking for her. I groan into my mug and regret leaving her to find her own way back. But it's been over ten hours and no one has knocked on my door. The likelihood that she survived is pretty high, right?

Over the next ten minutes, I push her out of my thoughts and make a mental list of the chores I have to get done today. Living the way I do takes planning, time, and most of all, effort. I don't run to the store for groceries. I grow my own food and raise my own livestock. Something as simple as heating my cabin has to be done by my hands. I spend hours a day chopping wood so when winter hits I'll have enough to get me through the season.

I toss my coffee cup in the sink and stare out the window that faces Avalon. It's a tiny speck in the distance, but it reminds me of her. When a fantasy of her moaning my name starts to take hold, I shake the thought from my head.

"Get a grip, Luke," I say. She's invaded my thoughts enough.

I head out into the crisp morning air, feed the chickens and other animals, and start on my daily task of splitting wood. The last thing I want is to be idle.

Sexual frustration courses through my veins, barely waning with every strike of the axe. I grip the handle tighter, swinging harder as she flashes through my mind. Images of her naked and the sounds of her moaning flood me like a seductive slide presentation only my sex-deprived mind could dream up.

Turning my face toward the sun, I wipe away the sweat that's starting to trickle down my temples. I silently curse my body and the woman who has worked her way inside my head. Even with my flannel unbuttoned, the cool morning air feels like a furnace blowing across my skin. Everything about my body is alive and burning with desire. My cock has stiffened to the point that I can barely think straight. Something has to be done about it before I end up cutting off my leg because I'm so fucking distracted.

I throw down the axe and stalk toward the cabin. I kick off my jeans and leave them on the bearskin rug in front of the fire before collapsing with a huff into my favorite chair. I grip my cock roughly. I give it a squeeze to settle it down and quench the dull ache that's plagued me since last night.

I lift my hips, chasing my hand with each stroke. The orgasm inside me builds with each pump of my fist. To get me there faster, I close my eyes and picture the moonlight sparkling off her naked flesh like a thousand diamonds set ablaze. I need this. I want this. I can almost feel her mouth wrap around the tip of my cock, languidly licking it as she moans in appreciation.

I grip hard. Pump faster. Straining to reach the orgasm that's just out of my grasp. Every time I get near, it eludes me. A tease within me—just like her.

"Hello," a voice says.

My heart stops, slamming against my chest like a truck hitting a brick wall at full speed.

My eyes fly open, and what do I see?

The object of my desire.

CHAPTER THREE

MADISON

I blink several times. There's too much to take in. The completely rustic interior of the cabin I've discovered at the end of the trail. The mountain of a man sitting only a few feet away, holding his massive cock in his hand. His golden skin glows and glimmers with sweat.

I'm shocked by what I see, and instantly aroused. I must be losing my ever-loving mind because my first instinct is to cross the room, strip off every stitch of my clothing, and impale myself on that glorious beast.

I blink again and swallow hard, but the fantasy doesn't go away. The man's gaze is hard and fixed on mine. He hasn't moved. His breathing is ragged, but he's frozen the fierce pumping motions on his cock.

An hour ago, feeling restless and no more ready to join the hippy club at the retreat center, I'd resolved to retrace my steps last night in the daylight. If I was going to respect nature as he'd wisely advised, I would have to get to know the trails better. So I'd followed the path to the springs, and then farther up the mountainside until I noticed the modest log-frame cabin set in a small clearing.

The door was open, inviting me in. Like a fool, I'd barged right in on the beautiful stranger from last night. The irony isn't lost on me that he'd caught me in the same precarious position only hours earlier. Maybe I should relish leaving him as frustrated as he'd left me, but I can't deny wanting to witness his pleasure.

A sharp pang of desire hits me between my legs when I imagine his release. Then I remember the way thoughts of him finished me off last night, and I wonder if he'd been thinking of me just now. My nipples harden painfully under my T-shirt, and despite the cooler air at this altitude, I'm heating up.

We exist in this silent standoff for what feels like several minutes, but might only be seconds. I can't keep count between the uneven beats of my heart and the fierce pulsing of all my pleasure centers. All the places I want this man's touch on me.

As if he can read my torrid thoughts, he makes the first move. A slow and languid slide of his fist along the length of his cock. My lips fall open. I lick them absently, noting how dry my mouth suddenly is. When I lift my gaze to his tan, rugged face, his clear blue eyes are trained on my lips. I lick them again, trapping my lower lip between my teeth. His lids lower slightly and his pace increases. In that moment, I realize my thoughts and whatever body language I've given off must have been loud as hell. We're in the midst of the most sexually intense silent conversation I've ever had in my life. And then I end it.

"I want you." The words rasp past my lips.

Before I can think about how insane I am or how desperate I sound, he's on his feet. His red flannel shirt flutters around his narrow waist before he pulls it off and stalks toward me, gloriously naked.

I take a small step back against the threshold, because he's huge in every way—his height and breadth, his fucking impressive girth, never mind the energy that seems to glow in a fiery ball all around him, threatening to consume me the closer he gets.

In another second, his arm circles my waist as he shoves the door closed with the other, trapping us inside the cabin. The only light comes through two windows cut into either side of the one-room house. I'm curious about the dwelling, but the sex god who dwells here demands all of my attention.

Not as gently, he pins my body to the door with his, and then his mouth lands on mine. I open immediately, because something about being in his presence is making me feel and do things that have nothing to do with careful reasoning. And deep down, I want him so fucking badly I can't make sense of it.

For all his brawn, the man's kiss is shockingly soft. I feel his strength in other places, like the hard grip that holds our bodies together and the firm press of his hips against mine. But his slow exploration of my mouth is gentle and passionate at once. His erection is pressing against me, flooding my mind with visions of what it could do, how good he'd feel.

I tunnel my fingers into his hair, loosening it from its tie as we continue kissing each other like passion-starved lovers. It's damp at the roots, rough against my fingertips, just like his unshaven jaw and the soft hairs that cover his broad chest. I find that I enjoy the sensation. The texture is like his scent—powerfully masculine, real, and raw. I want to lick him. Instead, I swirl my tongue feverishly against his. I trail my touch down his rock-hard body but slow my exploration at his hips.

I gasp for air, breaking the passionate lock of our mouths. As reason tries to break through, he takes my hand and guides it to his cock. I grasp it, noting its heat and my inability to fully circle it. His fingers curl around mine and guide me in a stroking motion that mimics his earlier.

"I want you too, beautiful," he mutters, his breath soft against my swollen lips. "I wanted you last night when you were spread out on that rock. I wanted you all fucking morning, so badly that all I could do was close my eyes, stroke my cock, and pretend it was you doing it. But here you are."

All the air leaves my lungs. It's useless. I'm a goner.

He shifts his thigh to rest between my legs, and I part for him. I moan when he adds delicious pressure to my pussy. I'd gotten myself off last night, but I'm wound so tight right now I could scream. I'd scream this man's name if I knew it.

"What's your name?" My voice is breathy, as foreign as this place and this beautiful stranger.

"Luke Dawson."

"I'm Madison."

His lips curl up a fraction. "It's a pleasure. Now that we're introduced, tell me exactly what you want, Madison."

He asks the question with renewed pressure on my clit. I curse inwardly, because *fuck*... Fuck is all I want.

"I want you inside me, Luke."

His smile retreats, and I swear the rings of blue around his irises darken. It could be the bad light in here. It could be the feral way he's looking at me before he goes for the button on my jeans, never breaking eye contact. He tears the zipper open with both hands and shoves the denim to the middle of my thighs along with my underwear.

Oh God, he's going to fuck me.

I'm terrified and more aroused than I've ever been in my life. I close my eyes and let my head fall back in surrender.

My eyes fly open and a cry tears up my throat as he plunges two thick fingers inside me. He withdraws, dragging across my clit on his way out. Then he brings them to his mouth, dipping them in slowly, like he's savoring the flavor of me. Everything inside me clenches. Luke Dawson is an animal, and so am I, because I've never experienced anything more erotic than his unabashed desire to taste me.

I'm trembling as he draws his fingertips, wet from my arousal and his tongue, across my lips before taking me in another savage kiss, sealing us together again.

With his other hand, he curls around my hand on his cock, reminding me how much I want his pleasure too. When I stroke him, up and down, he pushes his fingers deep into my drenched pussy again, and then retreats. In and out. In and out.

We move that way, creating a rhythm: stroking, fucking, breathing, pulsing, needing. Everything moves in sync and the world outside the cabin disappears. His touch is heaven and I'm immediately wild for more of it. The rhythm breaks up as we race to finish. My heart is speeding. He skips a beat to add another finger to his penetration. I'm struggling to give the full length of his cock the attention it deserves, from the thick root to the plush tip. He jerks and his abs tighten every time my thumb grazes over it. If I wasn't enjoying his finger fuck so much, I'd drop to my knees and take him in my mouth.

When his body tightens like a bow, I flick my gaze to his. The air presses out of my lungs when I take in the intensity of his stare.

"I'm going to come. You don't have to—"

I silence his next words with another deep consuming kiss and pump harder. I don't give a shit if he comes on me. I want to see it and feel it and touch it. The primal thought emerges from deep inside my lust-addled brain in a voice I barely recognize.

When he comes a few seconds later, his expression tightens into hard planes. His nails scratch against the rough wood at my back and his body turns into an impenetrable block of muscle. Watching him let go has officially taken first place as the most erotic moment of my life. Luke is...beautiful. I'm so entranced, I almost forget he's still three knuckles deep inside of me. He takes in a few steadying breaths before pulling back. I whimper when the movement leaves me empty.

He grabs his shirt off the light pine floor and turns back to me.

"Sorry about that," he mutters quietly as he cleans the warm sticky release from my hand.

All the while I'm standing here with my pants hanging down my thighs. He can't leave me this way. He's got to finish me.

He drops the shirt back to the floor and pins me with a wicked look. Something mischievous in his eyes makes my heart stutter. He must be able to read the desperation on my face because he smiles and presses a soft kiss to my lips.

"I'm going to take care of you, beautiful. Don't you worry about a thing."

Then he's on his knees, dragging my jeans down to my ankles and flinging them across the room. Before I can make sense of what he's doing, he's got my thigh hitched over his shoulder and he's buried his face between my legs.

The sensation of his tongue on my clit makes my head spin. I lift my arms and search for something to hang on to. They fall again and my fingers find purchase on his shoulders, and then into his mess of golden locks. My hips move with the undulation of his head as he works his tongue and fingers in perfect harmony.

His wide-mouthed assault draws long desperate moans from my lungs until my standing leg is trembling badly. Deftly, he slings my leg so my thigh rests on his other shoulder. He takes the full burden of my weight on his body like it's nothing, barely skipping a beat as he sucks and fucks me into oblivion.

"Madison. God, I knew your pussy was sweet. So fucking sweet."

"Oh God...Luke!" I'm so close I can barely breathe. And I want it so much. The ache is inside every cell of my body, clawing at me for release. I've never wanted anything so badly.

Then he curls his fingers inside me and I scream. The orgasm rocks me, strips everything down to a single point, leaving the rest of the world empty and flat and silent. My muscles go lax. Seconds go by as the world returns with color and oxygen and the warm buzz of release.

I flutter my eyelids closed with a sigh.

LUKE

I can barely register what just happened. I don't have time to work it out, because Madison is about to collapse. I maneuver her into my arms, tuck her against my chest, and bring her to the full-size bed in the back corner of the cabin. Her body flinches every few seconds while little breathy sighs keep falling from her lips. I fight back a smile, but can't ignore the pride beaming through me.

I lay her down on my unmade bed and cover her with a light quilt. For the first time since living here, I'm struck with a sense of insecurity about my living conditions. I glance around quickly, seeing it all through her eyes, even though they're presently closed. She'll rouse soon enough and see...well, not much. I exist with the bare necessities.

I wince. Not that I really care what she thinks. I mean, I'm glad that I made her scream my name, and coming with her hands on me was pretty much the best thing to happen to me in recent memory. But *she* walked into *my* cabin, uninvited and unannounced. So I'm not going to make excuses about my life when she opens her eyes and starts asking questions.

I shake my head, which is still buzzing both from my orgasm and the heady experience of burying my face between her thighs until she went boneless in my arms. I retrieve my jeans from their crumpled pile on the floor and pull them on. Madison is curled into my pillow, her lower half covered with the quilt. I briefly regret not stripping her completely so I might get another glance at her chest, which is now concealed by the simple pink T-shirt she's wearing. Heaven help me. If her tits had been bare, I might have come twice as fast and even harder.

My skin prickles with arousal. Goddamn. I draw my hand down my face, which only brings her scent into my lungs and makes my cock harden. Quickly and quietly, I move to my poor excuse for a kitchen and boil a pot of hot water for coffee. I'm not much of a drinker, but I am definitely drunk on this woman and I need to sober the fuck up.

I make the coffee and drink it, all the while staring at her slumbering peacefully on my bed. I'd never shared this space with another human soul. I feel like a part of me should be annoyed to be sharing it now, even for a little while, but I'm not. I like seeing her there. I love the idea of being able to walk over and push into her sweet cunt whenever I want to. Based on the earth-shattering orgasm I'd given her earlier, I don't figure it would be a hard sell. She'd open for me the same way she opened for me earlier. Mouth, legs, everything... She'd let me in before I'd even asked. She said she wanted me...

Warmth blooms across my chest and relaxes some tension I'm holding in my gut. My arousal is on a slow simmer that I can't quite turn off. And even though the possibility of fucking her in short order is at the forefront of my mind, she's sleeping and probably needs a little while to recover.

I stand, grab an old white T-shirt, and leave the cabin as quietly as I can. The sun warms the west side of the mountain. The air is dry and crisp. The only sounds are of nature. Just the way I like it.

I smile when I think about Madison's screams cutting through the constant soundtrack of birds and wind and the motion of the trees. Probably scared the fuck out of some of the nearby fauna.

I kill the next hour or so finishing the task that I'd been too wound up to complete earlier. I chop a good amount of wood, though I have plenty more to do over the coming weeks to compile all the reserves I want. My muscles are faintly sore, a sensation I relish. I like to use and push my body. I like to sweat and stand back and look at my achievements for the day, knowing the fruit of my labor will meet the needs of another day.

As much as I enjoy all that, I also can't wait to get back to the goddess in my bed. I tug my shirt off and wipe my body down of dirt and sweat before I go back. Maybe I can coax her down to the springs. We could get naked and clean and I could bend her over one of the rocks...

My hard-on quickly returns with that prospect, and I enter the cabin less quietly, hoping to rouse her if she isn't already awake. But the bed is empty. I dart my gaze around the small space. I scan twice more, pacing to the corners, as if somehow she'd miraculously turn up in the few hundred square feet of wall-less space. But no. She's gone.

CHAPTER FOUR

MADISON

The sound of his axe wakes me. Panic climbs up my back, seizing me. I blink slowly, trying to figure out if I'd dreamt the sound. Seeing the bare wood ceiling above me and smelling the unfamiliar male on the pillow tells me I hadn't.

It really happened. I walked in on him. I told him I wanted him. *Oh God.* Clearly there's something wrong with me. But instead of rejecting me, he took what he wanted without remorse, and I gave it to him willingly. I feel as though shame surrounds me like an unwanted blanket. I turn my head into his pillow and bury my face in it to groan softly. I'd never been so forward, so reckless with a perfect stranger—at least not while stone cold sober.

I lie there and stare at his nightstand for a full two minutes listening to the steady lash of his axe. Over and over again, the motion of his swings drifts through the window and creates a passing shadow in the bedroom. I pull myself up and sneak a peek through the window above the bed.

The beautiful wild man I now know as Luke Dawson looks more like a Greek god than a savage beast. His chest glimmers.

Points of light shoot off his wet, hard skin as his muscles ripple with each swing. A white T-shirt hangs from his back pocket, swaying and slapping him on the ass as he bends forward for another log. My mouth waters at the sight and wetness instantly pools between my legs. An hour ago, his fingers were inside of me and his warm, wet mouth suckled my clit like his very life depended on it. I should be sated. But I'm not. I want him again. I want to touch him once more.

I do the only thing that feels right. I scramble to my feet and search for my clothes. I grab my pants off the floor and then pull on my Chucks before taking a few seconds to scan the cabin. Luke lives simply without much in the way of material possessions. No television. No computer visible. No pictures on the walls. The cabin is like something out of a movie, and I can't imagine this being my life. In LA, I have all the comforts that money can afford me. Most I don't even need. The thought of having nothing but what sits in this cabin makes me question what type of man Luke really is.

I run out of there without so much as a goodbye, even after he gave me an orgasm that rivaled all orgasms I'd ever experienced. My brain is fuzzy from sleep and from Luke. I can't think of what else to do except make a quick escape. Hiding behind a large tuft of bushy pine trees, I yank on my pants without grace, barely doing it without falling over. I'd put my shoes on before my pants because I wasn't thinking clearly. Who could in my circumstances? Regret gnaws at my insides as I watch him searching the cabin in a fury.

Luke exits the cabin and begins to pace, running his hands through his long damp hair. His mouth is moving but I can't make out what he's saying. When he stops moving and turns in my direction, I gasp and take off. Not risking a look back, I push through the stray branches that reach out to stop my forward momentum.

I'm not even paying attention to where I'm going. I'm running out of sheer humiliation. I basically threw myself at him and begged him to fuck me.

Then the front of my shoe catches on a rock, and I go tumbling forward. Reaching out to try to break my fall, I collide with the ground. Tiny shards of stone break the skin, and my ankle twists in an unnatural way. My cries of pain echo through the thick forest and birds in nearby trees flee immediately. I cringe, drawing my bruised knees and battered hands inward. I feel my cheeks heat and tears sting my eyes as I lie in the rocky dirt.

There's a chill in the air I hadn't noticed before. I slowly exhale and roll onto my back. I close my eyes and try to even out my ragged breathing. I count to ten and wait for the dull ache in my knees and ankles to subside. When I finally crawl to my feet, a searing pain shoots through my right ankle, and I collapse under my own body weight.

"Fuck." I hiss, reaching down to soothe what I assume is a sprained ankle. "Fucking great." My voice is laced with aggravation at my stupidity, clumsiness, and most of all humiliation. I regret my decision to leave my cell phone behind in an attempt to stay unplugged during my stay at the Avalon.

I can't let him find me this way. Rescuing me in this condition after I ran like a coward wouldn't go over too well. At least I think it wouldn't. Luke doesn't seem the type of man to have patience in spades. Even if I have to crawl, I have to find a way back without his help. I'll give myself ten minutes to recover, and then I'll limp down the mountain back to Avalon.

But sitting idle gives me too much time to think about the ways my life has imploded recently. Jeremy did a smashing job at making me look like a complete fool. While I worked on the faces of Hollywood's elite, he decided to pick one of them to sleep with, effectively ending our marriage.

Tears sting my eyes and blur my vision. Using the back of my hand, I sweep them from my face. He lied to me time and time again, all the way to the end. I had to find out about the affair through a gossip television show. From that day forward, no one could look me in the eyes again. People felt sorry for me, ashamed on my behalf. I was never that girl. The one who needed pity from others. I'd come a long way in my life, relying on only my determination to succeed and ability to learn. But Jeremy wiped out my dreams in the blink of an eye—or in his case, with a pretty, young actress on the end of his dick.

When I signed the papers and freed myself from our relationship, Avalon was supposed to be a place of refuge. A spot for me to clear my head and get away from everything, including men. It would be just my luck that I happened upon a sexy lumberjack living by himself in the woods. But did I have to throw myself at him?

The branches overhead start to stir, and the wind whips up and cascades across my body. Shivering, I wrap my arms around my chest for warmth and comfort. With the quick dip in temperature, I'm liable to freeze if I don't make it to shelter tonight.

I stare up at the sky. The sunshine streams through the trees like the most intricate light fixture, and I release an exhausted sigh. I can't stay any longer. Like it or not I have to move. I wrap my arms around my knees and rock forward before I notice the blood soaking through my jeans. I hate to think of what could have happened if I hadn't been wearing denim.

"You can do this," I tell myself in a convincing tone that I almost believe. "You have to. Just get up and walk. Pain is a state of mind and can be overcome."

I laugh at my own cliché. Over the last few months I've read one too many self-help books. I know it's a bunch of bullshit. Not one thing in them has helped me get back on my feet—I'm doing it all by myself.

When another whipping wind penetrates my flimsy shirt, I push myself up and lift my right leg to baby my ankle. I grab onto a nearby tree for support and lower my foot to the ground, slowly letting my body get used to the throbbing pain shooting from my ankle and reverberating through my foot.

Just fucking fabulous. I have three options: stay here and freeze to death, yell out for Luke to rescue me and suffer his wrath for deserting him, or grin and bear it. Propelling myself forward, using the tree as leverage, I take a full stride.

"I got this," I say as my lips curve into a tight smile.

The thought of dying or facing Luke aren't viable options. I can only move forward. I hobble two steps and grunt. The agony that courses through my body is almost too much to bear.

"Damn it!" I yell out and crumble forward, using my knees as support.

Before I have a chance to straighten my back and push on, strong arms wrap around my waist and I collide with a hard chest. *Oh fuck.* I gasp in horror or shock, maybe a little bit of embarrassment too. I can't even bring my eyes to look at him. Staring at the shoulders that only hours earlier my legs had straddled, I do the only thing I can.

I whisper, "I'm sorry."

LUKE

There was nothing to say. Pissed off doesn't even begin to describe how I felt when I found the cabin empty. She disappeared without even saying a word. I wasn't keeping her prisoner, but I thought that the way I'd worshipped her body and tucked her into bed, I at least deserved a goodbye. But city girl Madison couldn't be bothered.

Instead of responding to her hushed apology, I bend forward and hoist her over my shoulder. I don't have time to talk. A spring storm is rolling in and there's a snow advisory at this elevation. For a second I debate which way to go—down the mountain to the resort or back to my place. The thought of having to explain why I'm carrying an injured woman back to the Avalon makes my insides seize.

"Put me down," she squeals and pounds her fists against my back.

I start the ascent toward the cabin. "Hush it." I swat her ass with a firmness that causes her to yelp.

She mimics the action, smacking my ass as she bounces in my arms. "You can't take me to your cabin. My room is the other way."

I keep on course and ignore her words. "Don't argue or I'll make you walk back." My voice comes out a little rougher than I anticipate, but she kind of deserves it.

"Seriously, Luke. I can walk."

She starts to wiggle in my arms, trying to scoot down my front, but I tighten my hold.

"I'm fine. I was just enjoying being one with nature for a little while."

"Save the bullshit for someone else, Madison." With each step, her tits bounce and crash against my shoulder blades, reminding me of their beauty and the reason I'm out here in the first place.

"Listen," she says, finally not fighting my hold. "You don't want me around and your cabin is the last place I want to be, so why not just leave me here and call the police, or security at the Avalon."

"No."

"Why go through all this trouble when you don't have to?" Every other word comes out at a higher pitch as her stomach collides with my shoulder.

"It's too dangerous with the weather that's about to roll in. I'm your only rescue until the storm clears." My feet dig into the dirt and propel us higher.

"Asshole," she mutters.

I hum, preferring the sound of my own voice to hers, and keep moving. As my steps carry us upward, the air grows colder. Dampness fills the air as the impending storm gets closer. She curls toward me and our bodies warm each other. I'm still angry and hurt, but my cock hardens at the contact. The scent of her arousal clings to me, amplified by her nearness. The familiar throb in my pants returns worse than before.

The cabin comes into view and she lifts her upper body to see my face. "What are you going to do to me?"

"Nothin'...unless you ask for it again."

"I did no such thing."

"I do believe you said..." My voice trails off. I laugh, deep and loud, to annoy her. "*I want you.* That's what you said, right?"

Her body crumples against my back in defeat.

"I didn't make the first move, Madison."

She sighs, burying her nose in my shirt and mumbles, "Well, I..."

"You walked in and said you wanted me inside you."

"I..." She moans softly, her breath warming my skin.

"Don't worry. It won't happen again," I tell her as I open the cabin door and walk inside with her still thrown over my shoulder. Using my toes, I peel off my boots, kick them toward the door, and cross the living room to the empty chair in front of the fireplace.

I drop her into it, and she instantly crosses her arms in front of her chest with a pout. Turning my back to her, I start to stack some logs in the fireplace. I can feel her eyes on me, boring holes into my back. When I strike the first match and toss it on the fire starter, she breaks her silence.

"I'm sorry," she whispers, repeating the words she first spoke when I rescued her.

I don't turn to face her. "For which part? Insinuating that I took advantage of you? Or for not saying goodbye?"

"Both."

The flame starts to grow, caressing the logs. Grabbing the iron poker, I jab the logs both out of necessity and frustration. Remembering the momentary joy I felt seeing her in my bed, my anger starts to simmer just like the fire. "Don't do it again. I did nothing to make you feel like shit for what we did. Don't make me ashamed of it either."

"Agreed." Her voice is soft and beckons me to turn.

She's glancing down at her blood-soaked jeans with a grimace on her face. Her palms are covered in dirt and dried blood like her pants. She would've never made it back if I hadn't gone after her. She would've frozen to death.

I push myself up. Her gaze follows me as I pull out a blue plaid flannel, a pair of boxers, and some socks. They're the smallest things I have here and the only things that have any chance of fitting her petite frame.

She stares up at me with her mouth gaping open but quickly snaps it shut as she takes the clothes from my hand. "You want me to stay all night?" Her eyes are wild and the fear I'd seen by the springs is back.

"There's a storm rolling in." I pitch my thumb over my shoulder toward the door, which is rattling from the wind outside. "No one will get up or down this mountain tonight. Whether I want you or not doesn't matter. You don't have anywhere else to go."

She balls her hand into a fist against her chest. "Where am I going to sleep?" Her lips are flat and her eyes narrow.

"Right in that chair. The fire will keep you warm, and I have a spare blanket around here somewhere. But first you need to change so I can look at your wounds."

Her head twists as she takes in the sparse surroundings that I call home. "Where?"

I laugh softly. "I've seen everything you got, Mad. Don't be bashful now."

"But, I..." She gapes at me.

Leaning forward, I place my hands on the armrests and cage her in. "I've tasted you too," I whisper with a grin.

She blushes and averts her eyes. "You're still a—"

I cut her off when I hover my lips a few centimeters above hers. "What am I?" I search her eyes and recognize the same lust she looked at me with earlier.

"Impossible." She smiles, obviously pleased with her own answer.

I raise an eyebrow, challenging her. "Is that all?" I lean in, ready to kiss her.

"Yep." She's quick with her response. Her eyes drop to my lips and her tongue darts out, sweeping across the ridges that I yearn to lick.

"Need help undressing?"

Her pupils dilate and her eyes darken, but instead of flinging herself into my arms, she says, "I can do it. Thank you." She jams her dirty hands in between us, breaking the moment. "Can I have a towel though? Hands." She wiggles her fingers for emphasis.

I nod and push myself up, trying not to seem disappointed. I don't know how I feel about this girl. One thing I do know is that she's fucking infuriating.

"Do you have a bathroom I can change in?"

I wet a towel at the kitchen sink and point toward the door near the bed. "Back there."

"I need to clean my hands and then I'll change. Okay?"

Handing her the rag, I study her closely as she sits in my favorite armchair. "Now you're asking permission?"

She glares at me and fists the damp towel in her hand. "Are you going to give me shit all night?"

"No, but right now it feels right." I stalk off, letting her scrub her hands alone while I start a fresh pot of coffee to help keep us warm.

"Ouch!" she cries out from behind me.

I turn and rush over to her, dropping to my knees in front of the chair. Wiping has caused the stones impaling her flesh to move and the fresh wounds are bleeding again. I pull the towel from her and reach for her hand, but she yanks it away.

"Ouch," she screeches.

"Gimme your hand. I'll be gentle."

Hesitantly, she rests her hand against my palm and seals her eyes shut. Slowly I blot the dirt away, paying careful attention not to make the bleeding worse. Reaching toward the coffee table, I grab my knife and start to move it toward the open flame in the fireplace behind me.

"What the fuck are you going to do with that?" Her eyes are enormous.

"Open up." The knife is in my right hand. The flames are flickering off the blade and sparkling on her face. "I have to dig the stones out and clean the wounds better so you don't get an infection."

She's holding her hand close to her body "Don't you have tweezers like normal people?"

I arch an eyebrow. "I'm a man, not a pussy. What the hell do I need tweezers for?"

"For splinters," she asks and her voice cracks. "I don't know. Most people have a pair for something."

I laugh and shake my head. "The knife is all I need."

"Said every serial killer ever," she mumbles.

I motion for her hand, but I haven't said enough to convince her. "I have survival medical training. I promise to do it as gently as possible."

"Where did you study?"

"Give me your hand and I'll tell you."

She groans, opening her hand with a pained look on her face. "Start talking."

I don't love the idea of telling her anything about me, but I use it as a distraction to keep her mind off the fact that I'm using a knife on her already tender flesh. "I learned how to treat wounds in the military."

"What branch?"

"Navy."

Her teeth clamp down on her bottom lip, and she starts to sweat. She's tougher than she acts. I know that although my touch is gentle, it still hurts. "You were a sailor?"

"Not exactly."

The dark wings of her eyebrows furrow inward. "What's that mean? Aren't all Navy guys sailors?"

"I was a SEAL."

My gaze flickers to her face for a moment before returning to the task, and her beautiful mouth forms a perfect O.

"For twelve years. Medical training was necessary."

"It was dangerous, wasn't it?"

"Sometimes," I lie, because every mission I went on was dangerous. SEALs aren't sent in for the easy missions.

"Were you scared?"

"Never." Another lie. Someone who has seen any type of battle and says they weren't scared at any point is a fucking liar.

I set her hand, palm side up, on her knee, and motion for the other hand. She's more willing to give it to me this time.

"How long have you lived here?" Her eyes start to roam around the cabin and for a moment I'm a bit embarrassed.

I drop my gaze to her hand and find that there are only a few pebbles lodged in this one. The other hand took the brunt of the fall. "Five years."

"Five years?" I can hear the shock in her voice.

"Yeah."

"Where are all your decorations?"

I shrug, but pay careful attention to my blade. "I don't need any."

"That's crazy."

I stay silent, pick the last stone from the fleshy part of her palm, and set the knife to the side. Finished, I lift her against my chest as I stand, but she stiffens.

I smirk. "I'm carrying you to the bathroom to change unless you'd rather do it right here?"

She relaxes, rests her head against my chest, and clutches the clothes against her stomach. "No, no. Thank you for carrying me so I can have some privacy."

"While you get dressed, I'll make us something to eat."

"Thank you," she whispers in a soft, sweet tone that's sincere. Lifting her gaze, she drinks me in with her deep blue eyes.

"You're welcome." I set her down near the sink and make sure she has a firm hold on the counter before removing my supportive hands. "Yell when you're ready."

She nods, shooing me from her. I spend the next ten minutes warming some stew I had stored in the cooler. I set out two bowls for us, and when I hear the bathroom door creak open I look over, and my stomach falls. I've never looked as good in flannel as she does right this minute. I want to drop to my knees and worship her exposed skin, taking my time peeling away the oversized clothing from her body before impaling her on my cock. But instead of doing that, I walk to her, lift her easily, and carry her to a seat at the table.

She lays the napkin across her lap. "Did you make this?"

"Yeah." I mimic her motion, resting a napkin against my leg before scooping up a spoonful.

"Mmm," she moans.

I close my eyes for a second and breathe deeply. "I'm glad you're enjoying it." I can hear the strain in my voice as I open my eyes. It's laced with lust and need and the tiny sounds she's making deep in her throat don't help.

"I am." She wraps her lips around the spoon and moans before pulling it out, licking it with her pink tongue.

My eyes focus on her luscious mouth and I push my bowl away, no longer hungry for food.

CHAPTER FIVE

MADISON

Warm orange flames lick up the blackened bricks inside the cabin's fireplace. The wind whips outside as the sky darkens to a midnight blue. Luke's figure passes by the window from time to time. He left his dinner unfinished to take care of some things outside before the storm comes in.

The thought had occurred to me that Luke might have exaggerated the danger of the impending weather to keep me here, but no part of me wants to take my bruised and banged up self down the mountain right now. Especially if snow is in the forecast.

I cringe inwardly and let my bandaged palms warm around the tea Luke prepared for me. Now I am alone with my thoughts. I was stupid for leaving him in such a rush. Now I'm paying for it with my injuries and having to face Luke for far longer than I'd expected.

He didn't deserve to bear the brunt of my confusion. He was a man—without a doubt, every inch a man—and I'd basically thrown myself at him. I'm not sure what I'd expected to happen. And even when I had offered him everything, essentially free reign over my body, he never made me feel cheap or ashamed.

My eyelids feel heavy. Maybe it's the tea, or my full belly, or being swaddled under Luke's quilt in front of a crackling fire. But even after my respite this afternoon, I feel as if I could sleep for hours more. I let my eyelids drift closed and the tension of the day, of my life, and everything that haunts me evaporates into the darkness.

◆ ◆ ◆ ◆

When I open my eyes again, only a dim amber glow lights the room. Hours must have passed, because the sky outside is black and the wind whistles through the invisible gaps between the logs more fiercely than before. I pull the quilt around me tighter, but the cold has already seeped into my bones. My fingers and feet are freezing. I squint and try to make out shapes in the room, but I can't see where Luke keeps the firewood.

I don't want to bother him, but the cabin will be frigid by morning if we neglect the fire. I blink a few more times and try to get my bearings before limping slowly toward Luke's bed in the back corner. I feel around in the dark, careful not to bust myself on the way. My knees hit the soft edge of the bed and when I reach down, Luke's body is warm under my hands.

"Is everything okay?" His voice is gravelly from sleep, and its texture resonates through me unexpectedly.

"The fire died. I can't find the firewood to get it going again."

"Shit, sorry."

He sits up abruptly and simultaneously pulls me down onto the warm place he'd just occupied. He launches himself toward the amber glow, and within a few minutes he's got it stoked up and throwing a heat I can already begin to feel.

He saunters back, his feet shuffling softly against the pine floor. The silhouette of his massive frame coming toward me has me pressing my knees together. He really is a sight.

"Thank you," I utter softly, gazing up at him.

Before I can rise and get back to the chair, he's on the bed beside me, pulling me down until I'm tucked against his chest and under a blanket we're now sharing. I shiver and sigh, because despite the cold air all around us, he's a furnace of warmth. I don't argue with his embrace, or his lazy caresses down my arms that end with my fingers warming up between his. I nuzzle against his neck and inhale, shamelessly reveling in his scent. The cologne designers have it all wrong. If they could bottle one hour of chopping wood, people would go nuts for it.

I should go back to my chair, but with every breath against his skin, every minute wrapped up in his heat, I soften and settle in. Something about Luke is a natural sedative—that is when he's not being a living, breathing aphrodisiac and driving me out of my mind.

I press my lips softly against his neck. "You smell good," I whisper.

He rises up on his elbow and stares down at me. Shadows play off his face as he smiles. "You smell good too." He lowers down and kisses my cheek gently. "You taste good too." With his free hand he traces a finger over my cheek and along my lips. "Only part I'm having a problem with is your mouth."

I frown, and his smile widens.

"Maybe it's the city girl in you."

"How do you know I'm from the city?"

"I wasn't born up here, you know. I've been all around the

world. I know a city girl when I see one." He continues feathering his fingertips along my jaw. "I don't know. Maybe it's just been a while since I've been around anyone."

I exhale and close my eyes for a long moment. "I'm sorry. I'm going through a lot right now. I'm not always this...defensive."

"Tell me about it."

I shake my head. Tension starts in my belly as I say the words, and the avalanche of my past comes down on me. "It's too much."

"I spent years witnessing things no one should ever see. I promise you can talk to me about anything."

Guilt rides over all the things I want to say. "That makes me feel even worse. I can't imagine what you've been through. I'm sure what I'm dealing with right now is nothing in comparison."

He's silent a moment before lowering his mouth to mine. The second our lips touch, my body comes alive. I slide my thigh along the roughness of his and hook it over his hip. Before I can fully entwine with him, he breaks the kiss.

"Madison, tell me."

I blink, trying to pull myself back to the conversation we were having.

"Listen," he says with a firmness that holds my attention. "You're hurt. That sprain won't heal for a little while. We'll have snow by morning, and I have no idea how long it'll take to melt so I can take you back down to the retreat. I'm happy to have you here with me, but if you're going to be a smartass from time to time, I'd at least like to know why. Otherwise I'm going to start thinking it's all me."

I imagine forming the words he wants to hear, and how it'll change how he sees me. "It's not you, Luke. I know this is my fault.

You don't have to take care of me, but I appreciate that you have."

He slides his rough palm up my thigh. "Let's think of it like a happy accident. Now talk to me."

I sigh and twist a falling strand of his hair between my fingertips. He's enough to take my breath away sometimes. But I need to just get this out. Rip the Band-Aid off.

"I finalized my divorce last week. It just hurts. We were together for a long time. Then, things changed."

I search his gaze for judgment, but his calm expression doesn't change.

"How long were you with him?"

"Since high school. We moved to Los Angeles together. Built up our careers. Before I knew it, I wasn't enough for him anymore."

"I'm sorry."

I shake my head. "I'm only sorry I wasted so much time. He is the only one..."

Luke frowns slightly, and I exhale a shaky breath. It's almost embarrassing to admit it in the context of Jeremy's infidelity.

"I've never been with anyone else. Can't say the same for him..."

Luke tightens his hold on my thigh and ends my confession with a kiss that leaves me breathless and on fire.

LUKE

I kiss her hard because I'm not sure how to process everything her confession makes me feel. I want to destroy the man who hurt her. What a goddamn fool. I want to erase him from her memory and eradicate the pain that I see in her eyes. I don't know Madison very well, but life is simple here. It strips away the unnecessary, the unimportant. I have a feeling that by the time I bring her back down the mountain, I'll know her soul. My first impression is that she has a kind one. She's strong too, but I need to strip down her defenses—the ones that sent her stumbling through the brush as she ran away from me without a parting word.

My own defenses kick in a little. I wasn't happy with her breakaway stunt, and as satisfied as she'd been after our little rendezvous, it hurts that she ran away so fast. Still, she lifts her hips, and I mold my palm to her ass, squeezing it appreciatively. I fucking love this woman's body. I'm not even trying to keep her from grinding herself against me. I want her too, but I need answers first...

I harness enough willpower to break our heated kiss and stare intently into her half-lidded eyes. "Why did you run away from me?"

Her gaze cuts sideways toward the fire, but I turn her back to face me. Her lips flatten, and I recognize the little flash of fire that comes right before she says something pissy. Just when I think she's going to, her lips soften. Everything softens and tears glimmer in her eyes as she begins to speak.

"Honestly, I wasn't thinking clearly. I have no idea why I feel so out of control when I'm with you. It doesn't make any sense for me to want you the way I do. I don't know if it's chemical or if I'm just such a mess right now."

"You're not a mess."

She swallows hard and tries to look away again. I guide her gaze back to me. I'm not letting her run away from me anymore. She huffs out a sigh before speaking again.

"I came to Avalon to get better, but I feel like maybe I'm just running away. I worry that when I go back home, I'll be the same.

Everything will still hurt like it does now. Maybe this is just a waste of time."

My jaw tightens. Somewhere inside her fear and vulnerability, I hear my own truth. I'd wrestled with those thoughts before. Was I running away up here? No, I couldn't survive anywhere else. This mountain is where I found my peace.

I push my emotions to the side, because Madison is the one hurting right now. And I fucking hate it. I need to take it away. I cup her cheek and hold her gaze to mine.

"Let me make love to you."

Her breath comes out in a rush. I want to steal the next one with a kiss. I could seduce her body, but I don't want her second-guessing her instincts and running away again.

"Say yes to me, Madison, and mean it. Then all you'll feel is me, worshipping you. I can promise there'll be no room for him in your thoughts when I'm inside you."

Her next breaths come fast and her body is toasty beneath me. Her little icicle toes are warm now and sliding up the back of my calf. I growl and press myself down into her a little. She's petite, and I don't want to crush her, but the way I want to slam our bodies together right now is almost more than I can bear.

"Do you have protection?" She utters the words that stop my lust dead in its tracks.

I shake my head. "Never had a need. Sorry, I guess I wasn't thinking either... It's been a long time for me."

She worries the inside of her lip with her teeth. "I'm on birth control. You don't have to worry about that."

Hope blooms around the non-starter of me not stocking my

cabin with a box of condoms I'd likely burn through over the next few days if I fucking could. I need to be inside her with a fierceness that makes me dizzy.

"It's your call, Madison," I say softly, sending a thousand prayers up that she says yes. I know I'm clean, and I believe she is too. But... "You've got no reason to trust me."

"But I do."

She slides her fingertips across my scalp and my balls tighten. I draw in a breath hoping it'll help me hold onto the last thin shred of my willpower.

"You've got to tell me now. Before I can't stop myself."

She arches and I press my fingertips into her flesh, drawing her tighter and closer to me. Need her. Need to get all the way inside her. Until she screams my name again, and again...

"Make love to me, Luke."

With a growl, I lift my hand to her collarbone, tuck my fingers under the flap of the shirt I'd given her, and yank hard all the way down. The snaps fly free, right along with my willpower. I pull the shirt apart and bare her chest. I don't waste another second molding my palm to her breast and massaging the plump flesh. She jolts a little and I pause, gauging her reaction.

"Your hands," she says.

I turn my palm up. The skin is slightly discolored in places where hours of manual labor have callused the flesh. I close my fist and curse inwardly. That couldn't feel good on her baby-soft skin. Before I can apologize, she grabs my hand, pries my fingers apart, and replaces my palm back against her chest.

"I like it."

I don't move, but she massages her fingers over mine, mimicking how I'd touched her before.

"I like the places where you're rough. Just startled me for a second. But I like it."

Something warms in me and I decide to believe her, until she gives me any indication to stop. I run my thumb over her dark nipples and lean down to suck one deeply into my mouth.

She moans, arches into the contact, and her legs shift restlessly around mine. I turn my attention to the other nipple, sucking it harder and longer, imagining how wet she's getting for me.

"More. I need more."

Heaven help me, I could post up at her tits for hours. Until the tips were reddened from my tongue and teeth and her flesh was swollen with arousal. But her throaty plea spurs me on. I lift to my knees and tug the boxers off her legs. Something about her wearing my shirt turns me on so I decide to leave it. I push my boxers down and spread her legs to rest on either side of my thighs.

My mouth waters at the sight of her cunt again, glistening in the faint light. Even with that proof of her arousal, I sink a finger into her heat and flick her clit until she bucks and moans. I need her more than ready for me. She's got a tight little channel for me to work my way into. I have no idea about the man who loved her and left her, but I'm guessing by the way she gawked at my cock this afternoon, I'm a lot bigger than he was.

She clenches around me and my patience disappears. I lower down, kiss her deeply, and nudge my aching cock against her opening. Slowly I push in. A low groan leaves my chest as her wet heat envelops me inch by inch. She sucks in a little breath and tightens, halting my journey to the end of her.

Her eyes are wide. "You're big."

I smile. "And you're perfect. You feel so fucking good around me."

She lets go of a sigh and a little bit of tension.

I brush my lips over hers. "Relax for me, beautiful. Let me in."

I thrust gently, feel her soften beneath me and give me the space I need to push all the way home. Once I'm there, she cries out and locks her thighs tightly around my waist. That's pleasure...and this is home. Right here. I thrust again and she's trembling.

I scan her features, frozen at the possibility that I have inadvertently hurt her. "Are you okay?"

She arches and drags her nails down my shoulder. "Don't stop. Oh my God. Don't fucking stop."

Relief and pleasure slide through my veins. Thank fucking God. After a few more tentative thrusts, I slam my hips hard against hers. Her lip trembles fiercely with the rest of her, and her pussy locks on me like a vise. Fuck me. She's coming already. Except this can't end yet. I ignore the burning need to come. Instead I focus on her. I study every expression, every desperate sound, and correlate them to the way I'm fucking her and touching her, memorizing what her body tells me gives her the most pleasure.

Nothing could satisfy me more. Almost nothing...

I've lost count of the minutes. Her orgasms bleed together and my own resolve starts to break down. I don't want this to end, but the promise of coming inside her is too sweet. The sensation creeps down my spine, giving me a little taste of how amazing it's going to feel letting go.

She slides her palms to my ass and squeezes. I lurch farther into her tight tissues with a groan. I catch her by the knee and push it up to her chest so I can fuck her deeper. Her jaw falls and our gazes lock.

"Are you ready, beautiful?"

"Yes."

The way she whimpers that single word makes me want to pull out and lick her to another few orgasms before I claim my own. Before I can follow that thought any farther, I'm driving into her so hard I swear I'm hitting something. She's holding onto the log posts at the head of my bed for dear life and screaming my name, coming hard for me one more time. It's the best sound...

Then I let go, and nothing has ever felt so fucking right.

CHAPTER SIX

MADISON

There's a delicious ache between my thighs as I lean back into his solid, muscular chest. Sitting on the bearskin rug in front of the fire and caged between his legs, I relish the feel of his body against mine. The flames flicker, glowing brilliant shades of yellow and orange, warming my front while he warms my back. He strokes his hand along my arm while nibbling at just the right spot in the crook of my neck. My fingertips feather up and down his legs in long, languid strokes. I close my eyes and revel in every sensation. His beard tickles my skin, sending chills down my spine and making my insides giddy. My body has grown used to his touch, expecting it and craving more.

The wind still swirls around the cabin and ice pellets have lashed the window panes for hours, but I don't care. I'm exactly where I want to be. Luke Dawson isn't the man I thought he was, especially when we first met. I had him all wrong. He's kind, thoughtful, and a generous lover.

In the last eighteen hours he's given me so many orgasms that every part of my body feels well used, even my toes from curling so much. Never in my life have I experienced a sexcapade quite like this. With Jeremy I felt like I had to beg, and that usually ended with a quickie standing over the bathroom sink before he jumped in the shower and washed the remnants of me away.

But not Luke. There's nothing fast about the man. He lives like he loves. My life is the total opposite. The moment I open my eyes in the morning, it's a mad dash to do everything that I have planned and all the things I haven't. Most days I forget to eat until I'm so weak that my fingers tremble applying a client's mascara, which is the least opportune time for a makeup artist.

The only thing Luke has been remotely swift with is his attention to me. If I shiver, he envelops me in his arms until the cold evaporates. If my stomach growls, he hops from the bed and fixes me something to eat. If I yawn, he carries me to the bed and whispers in my ear until my eyes flutter closed. He doesn't smother me with his actions, but makes me feel adored and important—something I'm not used to feeling anymore.

Little time has been spent talking. It's hard to ask questions when his lips are sealed over mine. But there's so much about him that I want to know.

"Luke." I open my eyes and tip my head sideways to give him full access to my neck.

"Yeah?" The deep rumble of his voice vibrates against my skin, giving me an entirely different sensation.

"Why do you live up here"—I swallow and pray I don't ruin the moment—"alone?"

He stills, but his lips remain against my skin. A moment passes before he speaks. "After I came back from my last tour of duty, I realized I didn't fit into mainstream society anymore." He's speaking softly, almost a whisper. His warm breath skids down my chest, causing my nipples to harden. "I came here because it's far enough away from everything and everyone that I can have some peace."

"But why not have a girlfriend?" I can't imagine being without some form of human contact.

He laughs softly and sinks his teeth gently into my skin before running his tongue over the same spot, soothing the burn. "Do you see a lot of women around here, Madison?"

"I'm here." I stiffen and start to backtrack. "I mean if I found you, so could others. Why not find someone to share this with?" My eyes scan the cabin. In reality there isn't much to share but each other.

"In the five years I've been here, you're the first woman to show up at my door and throw herself at me." He smiles against my skin.

"I did not throw myself at you," I say quickly and feel my cheeks heat.

"What would you call it, sweetheart?"

The term of endearment makes my embarrassment melt away and the ache between my thighs grow more intense. "I'd call it opportunistic. You needed help and I, being the caring and considerate person I am, offered myself for the job."

His laugh returns and his arms tighten around me in a warm embrace. "I had things handled." That he did.

I'd nearly swallowed my tongue when I walked in on him stroking his massive, hard shaft in his manly grip. "Be serious for a minute." I turn in his arms. My legs cover his and our bare middles meet once more.

His eyes drop to where our bodies touch. I touch his chin and force his face upward.

"Aren't you lonely here?"

"No," he answers quickly but frowns and tips his forehead against mine. "Yes."

"Which one is it?" I ask softly, resting my hand on his rock-hard bicep.

"I didn't think I was lonely before you showed up. But now that you're here..." He pauses and swallows roughly, his Adam's apple dipping underneath the hair that's smattered across his neck. "I don't know how I can go back to the way my life was before you came without feeling alone." I feel the weight in his words and the heaviness of his admission.

I slide my hand up his neck and nestle into the overgrown hairs covering his cheeks. "I'm sorry." It's the only thing I can think to say as I stare into his kind eyes. My heart flutters when I think about never seeing him again.

"Don't be." He wraps his hands around my back, the callouses scratching my skin ever so slightly. "This is the life I choose. I stay here because I have to, not because I want to. It's best if I live by myself so I can't fuck up anyone else."

The flutter in my chest stops and is replaced by a dull ache, because I know I've forever changed his life. "You're not fucked up, Luke."

"I am." He averts his eyes and presses his lips against my furrowed brows. "I'm more broken than you can ever imagine, Madison."

"What happened?"

"You don't want to know."

"Luke." I whisper his name like I've said it a million times. "I told you what happened to me, and I'll admit it was hard, but I felt like a weight had been lifted off my shoulders. Tell me what happened. You can't keep everything inside."

His hands slide under my ass, and he lifts me into his lap, cradling me against his chest. I'm not sure if he's doing this to comfort me or himself as he begins to speak.

"I saw things and did things that no man would ever be proud of doing or seeing. Even though it was to protect my country and done under classified orders, it doesn't sit right with me."

"Don't be afraid."

"As a SEAL, I was sent in to rescue people. Some people were held hostage and sometimes beaten to the point that they were almost unrecognizable. Sometimes it was a woman we were saving and she'd been raped. Ever look at a woman who fears you just because you're a man? To be looked at like a wild animal, to be looked at with eyes filled with so much hate you're certain she wishes you were dead instead of feeling comforted that you saved her life?"

"No," I answer honestly.

"I know what that feels like. It's shitty. Sometimes when I close my eyes on a still night, I can still hear the screams of children...and the wails of the families that lost loved ones. I saw too many things. Witnessed too much evil to ever be able to deal with the good."

"You're a good person, Luke."

His body stiffens under my touch. "I'm not. Don't be fooled by what's happened between us."

"You were serving your country. You aren't defined by those moments. We all have things we aren't proud of. Yours are just heavier than others'."

"That doesn't make it easier to swallow. When I came back, I moved to Denver. I lived in a high-rise and tried to make a life in the city. But everything set me off. When you go through something that makes you look over your shoulder, something like war, it's hard not to feel like everyone is after you. I started to remove myself from everybody, and when I couldn't deal anymore..." he trails off and buries his face in my hair. "I ran here. The only place I knew I could never hurt another human being."

"I can't imagine you hurting another living soul."

"I'm dangerous. I've murdered people with my bare hands, Madison."

His confession shocks me and the air rushes out of me in an instant.

LUKE

Instantly I regret baring my soul to her. I can feel her stiffening in my arms before she starts to pull away. I'd never confided in anyone before. Not even the therapist the VA required me to see. But there's something about Madison that draws me in and makes me want to admit my deepest secrets. The last thing I want is for her to be afraid of me, but she has to understand the man I really am—I'm not a white knight by any stretch of the imagination.

To my surprise, instead of extricating herself from me, she brushes the hair that's fallen in my eyes away from my face. "You've shown me nothing but kindness, Luke. You're not the man you think you are." Her palms scorch my flesh as she cradles my face. "What we've done in the past doesn't determine who we are for an eternity."

I wonder if she's speaking from experience.

"We're like rivers, handsome. We move through life touching different points and changing the landscape around us. But at our core, we're the same. We're water, dirt, and rocks. No matter what, that never changes. It doesn't matter if there's a flood or pollution flowing into our stream, we remain the same."

A slow smile spreads across my face as I stare into her eyes. I can't figure her out. The words that just came from her mouth are beautiful in their awkwardness. "You really are breathtaking," I whisper and sweep my hands across her back, needing to feel her softness against my toughness.

"You need to cut yourself a little slack. Honestly, I don't know many men who would come after me and rescue me after the way I ran out on you. Not even the ones who claim to be kind."

Flattening my palms against her skin, I pull her forward so she presses against my growing erection. "I would never leave you out there to die."

"That's because you're a good man, Luke." Her eyes twinkle in the firelight and her expression is soft and gentle like her tone. "Even though you probably hated me, you still saved me from whatever would have happened if I'd stayed out there all night."

"You would've died, Madison, and I couldn't have lived with that."

She searches my face. "Why don't you see your goodness?"

"I never felt especially good until I met you. I have this insatiable need to take care of you in every way."

She slides her hands down my throat, taking her time moving over my pecs before wandering to my abdomen and exploring the ridges. "Every way?" She raises an eyebrow with a smirk that tells me we're not talking about my past anymore.

"Every"—I lean forward, brushing my lips against her sweet mouth—"way." I kiss her again and she grabs my hand, moving it across her delicate skin to her wet and needy cunt.

"I need you inside me."

She makes a pouty face and pushes two of my fingers inside her. My cock stiffens underneath her to the point of discomfort.

"Fuck me, Luke," she begs.

My insides are burning for her, hotter than the fire warming us. Crushing my mouth against hers, I nudge her legs further apart and curl my fingers upward before pulling them back out. She moans into my mouth, sweeping her tongue deeper as if trying to taste more of me. My cock throbs as my fingers plunge back inside her. Her greedy channel convulses and pulls my fingers deeper.

I can't get enough of her. The way she moans at my touch makes everything else melt away. The words I spoke earlier are no longer important. The only thing I can think about is satisfying the beautiful creature in my lap.

I press my thumb against her swollen clit, circling around the tiny bud with the lightest touch to drive her wild as I fuck her with my fingers. She bucks against me, and I instantly want more of her—all of her. She's crying out, bouncing against my hand, and holding onto my bicep for support even though I have her cradled in my arms.

I need her orgasm. Need it more than the air in my lungs. Curling my fingers even more and pressing against her G-spot, I lift my hand slightly with each pass before thrusting into her with more force, matching her moans. Her fingernails bite into my flesh, breaking the skin as blood trickles down the back of my arm.

I'm too lost in the way she's kissing me and fucking my hand to care.

Nothing can stop me from getting her off. Plunging inside of her two more times, my thumb assaulting her clit and my fingers pushing up on the very spot that makes her scream with pleasure, I feel her body stiffen in my arms and her breathing halt. I drive on even though my cock is aching for the same attention. Then her body quakes with pleasure. Her fingernails dig deeper into my blood-stained skin, and I hiss into her mouth as she gasps for air.

"Watching you fall apart in my arms is so fucking beautiful."

She stares up at me with wonder and her body goes slack. Slowly, I ease my fingers out of her depths and bring them to my mouth, inhaling her sweet scent before closing my lips around them. The way she tastes on my tongue is better than any fruit I've ever grown. I close my eyes, savoring the lusciousness. My cock twitches in response.

Her breathing is hard, but she's still limp, studying my face as I lick every drop of her from my fingers. "I could taste you for eternity," I say in another moment of truthfulness, before my heart has a chance to pang in sorrow at the thought of her leaving.

"I would let you taste me always," she whispers.

Gripping her ass in my palms, I lift her over me before impaling her. Relief floods through me when I'm buried inside of her, but quickly I realize it's not enough. She rests her hands on my shoulders. When her body has adjusted, I slide my hands up her back, pulling her down and jamming my hardness even deeper.

Although I want to pound into her, my mind craves something

more…intimate. With her flush against me, I swivel my hips and don't break contact. Her pussy ripples as her head drops backward. A moan leaves her that I can only describe as pleasurable pain. There's nowhere for my cock to go but around, feeling every inch of her insides against the engorged tip. But I need more. I need to feel enveloped and consumed. Need to feel her mouth and steal her breath. I tangle one hand in her hair and bring her face to mine while holding her flush against me.

"Mad," I whisper into her mouth. "I need you. I need this." I confess because I've never craved anything as badly as her right now.

"I'm yours," she whispers in response and sweeps her tongue across my lips. I rotate my hips and move my cock inside her. "Take—" My hips move in the other direction and she sucks in a harsh breath before finding her voice again. "Me."

Her words are like a blow to my chest, and I'm momentarily rendered breathless until she grinds against me again. I swivel my hips faster, touching every bit of her, but it's not enough. Would anything ever be enough with her? I haven't found a way yet to tame the clawing need I feel when I'm in her presence. Moving my hands down her spine, I grip her around the waist and lift her from my cock. The way she whimpers at the loss makes me smile against her mouth before I pull her down, slamming her down on top of me.

I capture her screams and lift her up, repeating the motion with such force that I wonder if my hands and my thighs will leave bruises on her, but I can't stop myself. I'm like a wild man driven only by pleasure. My fingers dig deeper into her sides. I thrust up as I tug down, crashing our bodies together.

Desperate to see her, I drag my lips away from hers and study her. The fire shines on the thin layer of sweat that lines her body, sparkling like a million points of light with each movement. The tiny wisps near her damp hairline cling to her temples. When her eyes close and head tips back, her mouth falling open in the process, I feel my orgasm starting to build.

There's no time to savor the moment or appreciate her beauty. Not with the way my body needs the release. The sights, smells, and sounds are too overwhelming for me to quench the thirst I have for her except through my release. Pumping up harder, pulling down rougher, I scream her name as the orgasm grips my body and shakes me to my very core.

Overcome with so many things that I'm not used to feeling, I curl my face into her neck and try to fill my lungs with air. With every breath I suck in her scent, memorizing it for later. I want to stay here in this moment forever. But I know that she'll leave, and I'll go back to who I was before I found her in the woods, bathed in moonlight and sin. I hold her tighter against me, and as if she can read my mind, a single tear falls from her face and onto my shoulder.

CHAPTER SEVEN

MADISON

The sounds of the storm pelting against the windows are replaced by the trilling of birds. Snow drips from the trees and roof into melted puddles outside. Sunshine streams through the windows, adding warmth to our little refuge on the mountainside.

Luke and I sit across from each other at the small wooden table that fills out the kitchen area of the cabin, cards spread out between us. I furrow my brow as I strategize my next move. Luke lazily strokes the tops of my feet and calves, which are resting over his lap, using his other hand to hold his cards. We're playing best out of five, but I'm definitely taking this game of Gin Rummy more seriously than he is. Maybe because I'm naturally competitive. Or maybe because every time we make eye contact, something unspoken but powerfully intense passes between us. It's raw and filled with feelings that have crept over me the past few days. Feelings I wasn't expecting. When I let him inside me, I didn't expect he'd get this close to my heart.

But we don't talk about what this tryst means. We don't talk about the melting snow, or my healing wounds.

Suddenly, someone is pounding at the door.

I jump, yank my feet off Luke's lap, and stand up abruptly. I'm still hanging out in his flannel shirt, which most times makes me feel overdressed, but with a stranger behind the door, I'm suddenly feeling vulnerable.

Luke barely masks a scowl before rising and moving toward the door. He grabs a shotgun and opens the door. My heart thunders, but no one's ever made me feel as safe as Luke has.

I wrap my arms around myself. Not because of the gust of cool air that hits my bare legs when the door opens, but because we're no longer alone.

"Lou. What can I do for you?" Luke's enormous body fills the doorway, blocking my view of our unexpected visitor.

"Was wondering if you'd seen a girl up here. We have a guest down at the retreat and she's been gone since the storm hit. Indigo saw her head up the trail in the morning, but we haven't seen her and her phone's not answering. Her name's—"

"Madison. I know. She's here."

Luke interrupts the man gruffly, and moves to the side, allowing him entrance to the cabin. If I didn't know better, I'd think Luke didn't care for me too much by the way my name rolled off his tongue. But I suspect his tone has more to do with this visitor invading his space...and our time together. He props the gun beside the door and goes to the fire, staring into it wordlessly.

Lou is a much smaller and older man. He's wearing green hiking pants, a thick jacket, and a simple black ski cap that covers his ears. Salt and pepper gray hair sticks out over his ears. His eyes are bright and wide, and become even more so when he sees me.

"Well, you must be Madison. Good to see you, alive!"

He takes a few more steps in to shake my hand with a smile, seeming to pay no mind to my half-dressed body.

"Hi," I reply softly. "I'm sorry. I didn't mean to worry everyone."

"You did give us a scare. We weren't sure if you went into town, but we figured you might be close since your car hadn't moved. I rounded a few of us up the other night planning to hike up in the storm to look for you, but, well, it got a little worse than we expected. It was a tough call."

The anguish in that decision rested in the deep grooves lining Lou's forehead and his flattened lips. Suddenly I'm wracked with guilt. God, I'd been so stupid to think no one would care that I'd run off into the wilderness and holed up with a recluse for days. I hadn't expected to be away from Avalon for so long.

"I'm so sorry. I had no idea. I never meant to put you in that position."

Lou's worry lines ease a touch. "Don't worry yourself over it. All's well, and you're safe. That's the important thing."

I nod, because I've already apologized twice and even though it doesn't seem like enough, I'm struggling to explain my poor decision making. *Sorry, Lou. I was up the mountain having the best sex of my life while you were worrying if I was frozen solid somewhere on the trail.*

"Well..." Lou pulls off his ski cap and brushes a hand through his wiry hair. "The snow's not too treacherous anymore. If you're wanting an escort down the mountain, I'm happy to take you. Unless you're coming down soon."

I follow his gaze toward Luke, whose body has somehow turned to stone. He stands stock still, his arms folded thickly over each other, his legs wide. He's staring at Lou now with an unreadable expression. Then he shifts his gaze to me, taking a quick circuit up and down my body, before he turns toward the fire and shoves another log into it.

"Thanks, Lou. That'd be great."

My eyes widen. "But don't you—"

"Lou's right. The trail is safe now. Your ankle feels better, right?"

I can't speak. Another cold gust of air seems to have hit me with Luke's words.

"Your clothes are clean. I put them in the bathroom. You can borrow one of my jackets for the trip down. I'll come grab it next time I'm in Avalon."

My feet feel frozen to the rude floor. I can't escape the devastating reality that I'm being discarded, suddenly and abruptly. Why can't he take me down himself? When I'm ready...

But when would I be ready? The truth is that I don't want to leave. There's little to do here beyond fuck and eat and sleep and stare at each other, but I haven't minded it one bit. I swallow over the disappointment that's thick in my throat and move to the bathroom, closing the door behind me. I change into my clothes which have been carefully folded and set atop a wooden shelf that also holds a few mismatched towels. The knees of my jeans had ripped on my quick escape days ago, but have since been sewn back together with thick blue thread. Luke must have mended them at some point when I was sleeping.

My eyes burn. My throat prickles painfully. My stomach starts to burn and it hasn't for days. This is foolish. I'm a mess. He must have known it, and that's why he's turned his back so quickly.

But no matter what I tell myself about Luke, everything is

bleeding into feelings I have tried so hard to run from. Jeremy's words bang through my head as I dress with shaking hands.

We've grown apart. It's not you, it's me. I don't feel the same things I used to. It's not your fault. I can't be with you. It doesn't feel right. I'll always care for you.

Nausea races over the acid that's creeping up my esophagus. I can't let Luke know I'm hurting like this. I refuse to give him the satisfaction. We had fun. What the hell more did I expect?

"We don't see you much these days. Vi misses you. Always asking me how that Luke Dawson is doing. How about you come down sometime?"

"And do what, Lou?"

Luke's voice is low but Lou laughs. I still my rioting emotions enough to listen intently. Every time Luke speaks, I can almost feel it, like a rough pulse against my palms pressed warmly to the wooden door. I groan inwardly, because the thought of walking down this mountain away from him is almost unbearable. How can that be? Why... Why do I feel this way?

"Well, you could do the usual things. Get your provisions from town. Maybe circle back and spend some time at the main house. Vi makes a mean paella for the residents down there."

"I appreciate the offer, but I have no interest in getting spoiled."

"Sure, sure. Maybe we're not the biggest draw. There are some good folks who come through, though. Looks like you and Miss Atwood got to know each other a bit."

"I took her in from the storm. What did you expect me to do?"

Luke's words bite through me. I can't listen a second longer. I open the door and both men stare at me, each with a different brand of knowing in their eyes.

They can both go to hell. I'm not a victim. I find my sneakers by the door and tug them on. I'm almost out the door when Luke catches my arm and pulls a heavy jacket around me. I struggle, but I'm no match for him. Lou is out the door before I can say anything. He knows. He knows exactly what's gone on between us, and he's wisely given us space.

"Fuck you." I spit out at Luke as he zips up the front of the coat.

"Fuck me?" His strong jaw appears even stronger, his eyes cooler and harder.

"The first sign of life and you kick me out?"

"You didn't come here to be with me."

"But I'm here, aren't I?" I can't help how my voice wavers, how desperate I sound. Can he just throw me away so easily?

"I can't go down there." His voice is hard but tinged with regret.

"Why? Because you don't want to, or—"

"Because I can't!"

He shouts the last sentence and the tears that have been burning inside me break free. I swallow helplessly but they leak out of the corners of my eyes. *I hate you.*

I repeat the mantra that I've come to know so well. Except it's not directed at my ex-husband this time. It's all for this man who took me into his bed and discarded me just as easily.

I hate you, Luke Dawson.

LUKE

Madison marches out of the cabin, feet buried in snow up to her ankles, a few paces ahead of Lou. She goes in the wrong direction until he calls to her and she redirects to the path down. God, she's hopeless and I love her.

I can hardly breathe when I let those words roll through me again. What the fuck...

I shake my head and shut the door, cloistering myself back in the cabin. What I really want is some fresh air. It's warm outside, relatively. I've been holed up with Madison for days, feeding the fire, fanning the flames of my desire for her. I growl and shove a hand through my hair. Goddamn.

I scoop up the cards and tidy up the kitchen. Amazing how messy it gets with a woman around... A woman I can't keep my hands off of. It's not practical. Not what I came up here to do. I was falling too deep.

I don't bother pulling on a coat before I go outside. I shovel a path all around the house. Shovel to the places where work needs to be done. Heavy thick snow. It'll be water and mud in another day. I don't know why I bother. But I need to burn. I have to get my mind off her. Because I can't go down there.

I hate going to town. I walk into the general store, and they all stare. It's like they know. They know I don't belong in society. Not that the people of Avalon wear any airs, but I'm not fit for a small town or any town. I'm not fit for a city girl like Madison. Sure, fucking her was one of the best experiences of my existence, but that's the man in me talking. The man who hasn't been with a woman in years. Doesn't matter how soft she is when she moves against me, the sounds she makes when I'm deep inside her, or the easy way we are when it's quiet. Soon enough she'd want more. My life in the cabin isn't a life anyone else wants. Best to send her off before I get even more attached.

Even as I rationalize this, I can't stop thinking about her. I'd made love to her first thing in the morning. Only hours ago I'd tasted her pussy as she sighed and groaned into consciousness. I'd taken my time exploring her with my tongue and fingers, ignoring my erection. I remember thinking, *I could wake up every morning this way, worshipping her gorgeous body in my bed*. When I couldn't hold out any longer, I'd spread her wide and fucked her slowly and thoroughly until she was begging me to take her hard to the finish, which I did. Her tight little body could always take all of me. And the look on her face when she came...

I throw the shovel against the side of the cabin and march inside, cursing along the way. Despite being alone so long, I'd accepted and welcomed her into my life without hesitation. What a fucking idiotic thing for me to do.

I've been lonely before. Plenty lonely. But it's always been a manageable discomfort. Doesn't hurt like the past. Doesn't hurt like judgement and reliving memories of war. And fuck me, it's never hurt as much as watching her walk away from me. But I can't let it get to me.

My time with Madison was a fleeting gift. Like a dip in the springs. A warm little haven. But only for a while. My home is here... and her home is in the city.

CHAPTER EIGHT

MADISON

Pushing the paella around my plate, I try not to think of him. Just when I thought I was finding my footing again, he ripped the rug out from under me and gouged open the wound that Jeremy had given me—a wound that was just starting to heal.

I hate him. I was a fool for believing that I meant anything to him. I was just his plaything, something to pass his time in a freak spring storm.

"What's wrong, Ms. Atwood? Do you not like paella?" With my head down, all I can see are Indigo's ankles.

I stab a chunk of chicken and plaster a fake Hollywood smile on my face before looking up. "No, it's actually delicious." I close my lips around the fork and pray she doesn't have anything else to say. Indigo's sweet, but I don't feel like talking to anyone right now. "Mmm." I smile, chewing quickly.

"Oh, good." She pulls out a chair and it takes everything in me not to groan. "I heard you got lost in the storm. I'm so happy you made it back safely." She's rattling on and barely takes a breath before she continues. "You could've really been hurt."

"I made it back safe."

"Yep." She leans forward, placing her hands on the table, and lowers her face. "There's a rumor I want to ask you about," she whispers, her eyes peering around the room.

I brace myself, expecting a question about Jeremy to come sliding off her tongue. "Sure."

"Well," she whispers, licking her lips as she does a second sweep around the room. "I heard that you were rescued by the man who lives on top of the mountain. Is that true?"

"Yep." My tone is clipped. Dredging up what happened the last few days is like rubbing salt in an already aching cut.

Her eyes widen. "What's he like?"

"He's..." I pause and wonder just how much I want to share about him. If I say too much, especially the nice parts about how handsome he is or what a generous lover he can be, every woman in a fifty-mile radius will try and get lost on that mountain. If I say what I'm really feeling, that'll spread just as quickly but also probably get back to Lou, which will eventually bleed back to the asshole. "He was nice," I say simply, and leave it at that.

She dips her chin and cocks her head. "Just nice? Huh."

"Yep. He's nice." My teeth are clenched and my jaw aches as I continue to fake the biggest smile I can muster.

"Is he hot?"

"He's all right, I suppose," I lie with a straight face. "If you go for the long hair, overgrown facial hair, caveman look."

"Thanks!" She pops up from the chair and tucks it back underneath the table. "Just wanted to check on you. I hope you have a good night, Ms. Atwood."

"Bye." I give her a quick wave.

My words were meant to not make him sound sexy, but as I sit there and replay them in my mind, I know I screwed that up. Her face lit up when I said it, and I couldn't take it back. Indigo and probably every other single woman around here would find him sexy.

This isn't LA after all.

Hell, who am I kidding?

Even the women in LA would find that description intriguing at the very least.

Instead of singing camp songs by the fire after dinner with the rest of the retreat guests, I return to my room and lock myself away with my thoughts. It's the first time I let myself really process what happened.

After I made my way down the mountain, with Lou close on my heels but giving me enough space to be alone, I felt almost too much anger to see straight. As soon as my head hit the pillow, I'd drifted to sleep and dreamt of him. But the call to dinner came too quickly for me to have a chance to rehash all of the events of the last few days.

Alone in my room now, sitting on the edge of the bed and staring out at the mountain—his mountain—all I can do is think of him. He lured me in with his gentle strokes and soft kisses. I believed that I meant more to him than I did.

Maybe the part of me that was broken and ripped apart by Jeremy made me need to believe, but that same part betrayed me in the end. Luke was the strong, silent type my body and soul craved after spending years with a needy, ungrateful husband. Somehow, over those few days with Luke, the sting of Jeremy's affair and our divorce no longer made my heart seize inside my chest.

Luke had held me, thrusting into me with purpose and care. He never made me feel cheap. The very thought of his mouth on my skin makes desire pool between my legs and the flames of arousal lick up my spine. I want to go fight with him and tell him he's wrong— he doesn't have to be alone. But I stay where I am and try to forget everything about him. It's better for both of us to chalk it up to a great lay brought about by circumstances out of our control. Right?

Unable to sleep and still not interested in the Kumbaya shit happening down in the clearing, I walk casually to my suitcase and grab my laptop, which I swore I wouldn't open during the entire trip. I press the on button and plop down on my bed.

Stretching out on my stomach, I log in. I tuck a pillow underneath my chest while I wait for all the programs to load. First, I open my email. I quickly realize my mistake. My inbox is flooded with messages that all have a subject line that includes the word Jeremy. Dozens of reporters are asking for interviews and some of them are offering big money just to talk to me about my ex. I close my eyes and take a deep breath before closing my email and forging on.

Jeremy will not affect me. He's no longer part of my life. Even though he did me wrong, the last thing I want to do is open up about our past and see it replayed on television and in newspapers for years. I'm done with that part of my life and refuse to let anyone interested in gossip or profit reopen that closed chapter.

Next, I check my social media threads, preferring the dramas of others to my own. When the first photo of him and her lands in my newsfeed, I drop my head down and curse into the comforter. "Motherfucker," I mumble. "I hate them both."

After quickly unfriending the person that posted the "newly engaged and happy couple" photo, I decide it's time to start over, right down to my clothes. The old me is gone. The victim of a husband who didn't love me the way I deserved. I'm ready to throw away the old and became a better version of my former self. I spend an hour shopping online, purchasing an entire new wardrobe. It's the first step in my plan to change my life.

My thoughts float back to Luke, the man who has me so angry that I can barely see straight. Who is he? What made him want to remove himself from society? I have nothing to go on besides what I know from the amount of time I've spent with him. Like how his cock feels against my lips, how his hands caress my skin, how many times I can orgasm against his tongue, and how he sounds when he comes and moans my name.

So I do what any slightly obsessed and angry person would do... I Google him.

LUKE

Silence. It used to comfort me.

That was before Madison turned my world upside down.

Pacing around the cabin, I drag my hands through my hair and clench my teeth so tightly my jaw starts to ache. There's no other sound. No sexy laughs from Madison. No moans in the throes of passion. There's nothing except my boots scraping against the wooden floorboards and the maddening drip of the snow melting into puddles outside the front door. The peacefulness of the cabin that used to soothe me now taunts me.

I couldn't just leave her out there to freeze to death. When

I found her, I thought I could have her here, invading my world, without any lasting effects. Dumbass me thought I could handle a few days alone with a beautiful woman and come out unscathed, right? What a fucking idiot I've been. I tasted the woman. I fucked her. I knew what it was like to be nine inches deep, thrusting into her with everything I had and hearing my name come out of her mouth in screams as I fuck her like she's never been fucked.

I slept like shit last night without her in my bed. I tossed and turned for hours, pleasuring myself more than once as I tried to force myself to sleep. When I finally drifted off, she haunted my dreams. The feel of her skin. The taste of her mouth. The smell of her hair. The way she smiled at me. Every memory tormented me and there was nothing I could do to stop them.

Walking outside, I pull in a deep breath of cool spring air and shield my eyes from the sun with my hand. I scan my surroundings. There's barely any movement besides the rustling of leaves and birds singing in the background. The stillness of this place is amplified without her presence. Instead of calming me, the silence sets me on edge.

"Fuck." I groan, dragging my hand down my face.

Madison did nothing wrong. She confided in me about her ex-husband, so I knew she was fragile. But like the asshole I am, I threw her out without even thinking.

Only one thing can remedy my fuck up. I have to trudge my ass down the mountain and find her. I avoid Avalon at all costs except when Lou and Vi need to speak with me or when I have a concern over the use of my land. I've only gone there on slower days, when new guests were checking in.

But today isn't that day. I push the thought from my mind as I start down the trail that Madison walked yesterday. My heart beats a little faster with each step. My body craves her, coming alive as if it senses her nearness. Voices coming from the hot springs draw my attention, and for a moment I wonder if Madison is there. I almost turn around to see if the laughter is hers, but my instincts pull me the other way.

When I finally make it to the clearing, it's worse than I imagine. People are everywhere. Yoga classes are taking place on the expansive wraparound back deck. Five people are sitting near the simmering fire sipping coffees. Others are strapping on hiking gear.

A few ladies smile in my direction, their gazes slowly moving up my body before finally landing on my face. I give them a quick, awkward nod, but move forward.

"Luke!" Lou's voice breaks through the chatter of the resort guests. "Over here," he says.

I turn in a circle to get my bearings. He's waving me over with an axe in one hand and a lopsided smile on his face.

Lou is harmless. He's one of the only people I like and respect around here. Yesterday I was an asshole to him too. Not because I don't like him, but because he interrupted the best few days I'd had in a long time. I knew I couldn't send him away and keep Madison by my side.

"Lou." I greet him with a firm handshake.

"What brings you down the mountain?"

"Well, I..." Suddenly uncomfortable, I tuck my hand in my pocket and pause.

Hoisting the axe over his shoulder, he tilts his head and studies me. "Coming to see Ms. Atwood?"

My palms start to sweat and a knot forms in my stomach. I hadn't thought about how Lou and Vi would feel about me coming to see one of their guests. "I just wanted to make sure she's okay."

He grabs a log from his pile, rests it on the chopping block, and swings the axe down, splitting the log in two. Without missing a beat, he says, "You two looked mighty cozy."

"It's not what you think."

He chuckles softly.

"I fucked up, Lou."

"Probably," he says quickly. "Women aren't like us, Luke."

I grab a log, placing it on the block for him. "I'm learning that. I have to make it right with her."

"Groveling will help."

I laugh this time. I haven't groveled my entire life and don't know if it's something I can start doing now. "Sounds easy," I lie.

The tiny crinkles near the edges of Lou's eyes deepen when he smiles. "It can be, but it's hell on your ego."

I quirk an eyebrow, amused with the old man. "You grovel a lot?"

His lips flatten as he slowly nods. "Couldn't stay married this long without eating a few slices of humble pie."

"Good to know." I pause for a moment, but I can't chit chat anymore. I need to find Madison and make things right.

But Lou keeps on. "Remember *you're* wrong, *she's* right, and it'll always turn out in your favor."

"Got it."

He wipes the sweat from his brow. "I don't usually give out guest information, but I think Ms. Atwood would like to see you. She's in the Olive Annex in room 121. You know where that is, right?"

"I think so."

"Stop at the front desk and ask Indigo to guide you. She has dreads. You can't miss her."

I take two steps back, growing impatient knowing she's so near. "Thanks, Lou."

"Good luck."

When I pull open the door of the main building, I brace myself for whatever weird stares and comments I may hear. Although they're in the wilderness, most of the people here are well dressed and not used to someone as country as me. To my surprise, only a few people are sitting on the oversized leather couches in the middle of the three-story lobby.

When I approach the desk, a woman, who I assume is Indigo by the long dreads Lou described, is typing furiously on the keyboard. She doesn't look up. "One moment. Let me just finish this." Her tongue darts out, and she narrows her eyes on the screen.

"No problem." I take that moment to take in the majesty of the Avalon. Lined with wood beams and tribal art, the Avalon's beauty is almost breathtaking. I'm so caught up in taking in my surroundings that I don't hear the desk girl stop typing. "Oh," she says. "Um."

"Hi." I clear my throat as uneasiness creeps in.

She snaps her mouth shut and gazes at my face. "Can I help you?"

Placing my palms on the counter, I grip the edge, needing a little support to keep me from fleeing. "Can you tell me how to get to the Olive Annex?"

Her eyes haven't left mine, but there's a blush climbing up her neck. "Sure." She darts her tongue out again and a tiny silver ball slides across her top lip as she gazes at me, almost undressing me with her eyes. "Wait a minute. Are you here to see Ms. Atwood?"

"Yeah." Uneasiness settles in the pit of my stomach. "How did you know?"

"You're quite the topic of conversation around the retreat. We don't get any true mountain men in here. Just wannabes. You're hard to miss, and I mean that in the nicest way."

"Oh." I smile awkwardly. "Thanks."

"I'm Indigo." She motions to her name tag hanging just above her breast. "It's nice to finally meet you, Mr. Dawson."

"You as well." *I can do this.* I can be personable in spurts. For Madison. "So... Can you point me toward her building?"

"She really didn't do you justice. I mean she said you were okay looking, but holy cripe, she was holding out." She rattles on and her eyes slowly travel from my arms to my face. "She never said you were the real live Paul Bunyan himself, but a whole lot sexier."

Heat creeps up my neck out of embarrassment. But the one thing I do get out of her rambling is that Madison has talked about me. "Well, thanks. And her building?"

"Oh, sorry. I kind of get sidetracked sometimes." She grabs a map from next to her keyboard and slaps it on the counter in front of me. Leaning forward and getting as close to me as her tiny frame will allow, she draws a circle around one of the buildings. "It's just a short walk if you follow my arrows." She draws two large arrows with a sharpie. "I can walk you over if you'd like."

"No, I appreciate the offer, but I think I can find it."

"Sure. Silly me," she says and rests her head on her palm, staring up at me with wistful eyes.

Indigo is sweet. Back in the day, before I became the man I am now, I may have flirted back. But now there's only one person who has my attention, and she's just a few feet away.

Indigo laughs nervously. "She's going to be so excited to see you."

"I'm sure," I mumble and straighten, needing to put a little space between us.

I start to walk away when she comes around the desk with a business card in hand.

"In case you ever need anything. We're always here to help, even the locals." She jams the card between us.

Instead of being my usual asshole self, I take the card and shove it in the back pocket of my jeans. "Thanks. I'll keep that in mind next time I need something."

"Sure. You have yourself a good day, Mr. Dawson."

"You too."

With each step toward the Olive Annex, I practice what I'm going to say to Madison when she opens the door. "Maddy, I'm sorry." I shake my head. "Too simple."

I push open the door and walk outside. Her building is only a couple dozen feet away. "Maddy, forgive me." But the words still don't seem right.

Lou said I need to grovel, but I'm not used to talking to people, let alone apologizing. Instead of figuring out what I'm going to say, I concentrate on my breathing and remaining calm with each passing step. The words will come to me, or at least I hope they will. I don't want to sound like a robot when I finally see her.

I shake my hands and arms, trying to rid myself of the nervousness that's gripping me. "You can do this, Luke. You have to do this."

I square my shoulders, take a deep breath, and knock.

CHAPTER NINE

MADISON

I'd spent over an hour reading everything the Internet had to say about Luke Dawson. War hero, land owner, and according to a long-abandoned Facebook account, a totally normal guy before he joined the service. Tears stung my eyes when I'd clicked through photos of a far less rugged and much younger Luke, hanging with his friends from school, standing beside his parents after graduation, and taking selfies with his fellow sailors. Then nothing.

Just the land titles for the very property I was sitting on, an impressive acreage that would make anyone else wonder why he chose to live on the small patch of land where his one-room cabin sat. The stories of his service resolve more with the man I know—the intense, hardened man who'd worked his way into my heart in only a few short days. He'd been honorably discharged after receiving the Navy's Silver Cross for acts of extraordinary heroism during his time served. The details were vague and likely classified, and Luke's quoted remarks were brief and hardly quotable, like he didn't want to own any part of it.

A part of me wished I hadn't gone snooping. Hating him had

been much easier when I knew less. Now I sit on my bed, stunned by the truth and suddenly full of doubts. The sun drifts behind the mountain, and the sky through my sheer curtains slowly fades into night. All I can think about is wanting to give Luke Dawson the benefit of the doubt. I know he's been through more than I could ever imagine. Maybe he's socially awkward and hell-bent on isolation for reasons that seem strange to the rest of the world. But maybe they make perfect sense to someone who's been through his kind of hell.

Isn't that why I was out here, after all? To escape my life, my past...my own personal hell? I squeeze my eyes closed, but it doesn't relieve me of the image of Jeremy and his new fiancée. I thought a month away would do me good. I realize now no amount of time will take this hurt away. I can run, but I'll have to go back home eventually, and as long as Jeremy is there, I'll have to face what he did to me.

Damn it. Maybe Luke has it right. Maybe I just have to find my own mountain. Except mine won't have a beautiful stranger on it to make me feel safe and special and...

I sigh and let my head fall back into the pillow. Missing him more than I should, I glance out the window again, and for a split second I swear I recognize the outline of his body. My heart does a little flip and then the reality that our fling is undeniably over sinks in.

I'm ready to drive into town and find a bottle of wine with my name on it when I hear a knock on the door. I rise and walk barefoot across the carpeted floor to answer it. I open it, blink rapidly, and swallow over the knot of emotion that's suddenly clogging my throat. Goddamn, Luke looks better than ever somehow. Had I missed him so much?

Before I can say anything, he's got his hands on either side of the door frame and a look on his face that I've never seen before. Hard and determined.

"I'm sorry," he says gruffly, a frown marring his brow.

"You're sorry?"

"Yeah." He stares down at the ground and then back up at me. "I shouldn't have let you leave."

I swallow again, but my nerves have taken over. What is he saying?

"You basically kicked me out the door."

"It was a mistake. I told you I was sorry."

His frown deepens, and I resist the urge to smack him.

"Do you really think you can just come here and—"

I can't finish, because his hands are cupping my face and his lips are sealed over mine. His taste floods my mouth. His earthy scent permeates the air between us, revving me up and calming me at once. I take two fistfuls of his shirt and he pulls me closer. My thoughts scatter and my flash of anger fades, morphing into something else— passion that I'd been missing since I left his cabin.

He kisses me fiercely, breaking contact only long enough to whisper that he's sorry a couple more times. Every time he says it, my heart breaks... Or is that my heart healing in the places where it'd been torn?

All I know is that I'm glad he's here. Together we move into the room, and he kicks the door shut behind him. He's everywhere, like a warm blanket that enveloped me the second he walked in. My brain can hardly catch up with being in his presence again so suddenly.

"Luke," I gasp his name, trying to slow down the rush of emotion overtaking me.

He doesn't answer. He only tugs off my shirt and then his, so our skin touches. I exhale a shuddery sigh at the pure relief of the direct contact, my breasts pressed tightly against his hard chest. *I belong here...with him.* I can't possibly overthink it, because it's my heart talking, loud and clear. All my instincts seem to be chemically wired to my attraction to this man.

I trail my shaky touch down his chest until I can unfasten his jeans. His abdominal muscles tighten and jump against my fingers. I'm about to free his cock when he spins me and bends me over the bed. He yanks my jeans and panties to my knees, and a low moan leaves my lips.

I curl my fists into the bedspread and brace myself to take him into me when he molds his body against the back of mine. He kisses my shoulder and licks along the line of my neck, eliciting a whole body shiver. I bite my lip to keep another moan at bay.

"So beautiful," he whispers.

He grasps my breast and lines his cock up, pressing into me inch by inch. He slides in easily, with no resistance. I got wet the second I opened the door and heard his voice again, and now I'm wild to feel all of him.

He roots deeply and I cry out, tightening my grip on the bedspread.

"Do you forgive me, Madison?"

Oh, what a bastard he is. Not fair. Not fair at all. He thrusts, and I almost forget the question.

"Maddy, sweetheart. Talk to me."

"Yes."

He hooks his arm around my hips and thrusts again, harder this time. I can feel my orgasm building already.

"Say it, sweetheart."

"I forgive you," I whimper. "Now please, fuck me. I need you. Please..."

He says nothing, and I pray we're done with words. I'd nearly forgiven him before he knocked on the door. I'd drop to my knees and beg for anything now.

I expect him to launch into fierce drives, but even in this position, which has always made me feel exposed and vulnerable, I feel like he's loving me, carefully, deliberately. He gives me what I nearly begged for, all the while caressing me. Up my back and between my shoulder blades. Down over my hips, and to my front where he toys with my clit. I could never confuse Luke's touch with anyone else's. Never in a million years. His tenderness is unmatched, and the rough trail he draws over my skin adds a different kind of awareness to every touch.

For all his tenderness and slow strokes, I'm riding the edge of an orgasm before I can talk myself out of it. The way he grips me and speeds up his ministrations tells me he's there too. A little time apart, and the fuse is too short. I cry loudly into the bedspread, hoping the walls aren't too thin. He follows me down, moaning my name into the air with one final punch of his hips.

LUKE

I gulp in several breaths. Jesus, if the whole retreat didn't already think we were fucking, I may have just removed all doubt. I'm pretty sure we were loud, but as I slip out of Madison's beautifully wet cunt, I could not care less. I'm buzzing from coming so hard, and her acceptance of my dozen or so apologies is icing on the cake. In this particular second, everything is right in the world.

She turns, resting her bottom on the edge of the bed as she toes out of her pants the rest of the way. I shake my head, because I can't seem to get over how beautiful she is. If she wasn't dripping with my release, I'd spread her out and suck her to a few more orgasms, because worshipping her body is fast becoming my favorite thing, ever. My cock twitches with the mere thought.

"Come on." She rises and takes my hand before leading us to an adjoining bathroom.

She turns the shower on. I'd reviewed the blueprints for the retreat years ago, but I've never been in one of the rooms. Everything feels odd about this, except that I'm with Madison, and that pretty much always feels right.

She turns and runs her palms up my forearms, gazing up at me. "Everything okay?"

I nod quickly. "Yeah. I just... I'm not used to this."

I gesture through the room. She lifts an eyebrow.

"Like, running water? Electricity?"

I shrug. "Maybe."

She smiles and steps into the shower. I follow her and the water pours down on us. It's hot like the springs and that makes me smile a little. She folds her arms around me, and we stand that way for a while, in comfortable silence. The fluorescent lighting of the bathroom is vaguely irritating, and I'm missing the security of the life I know, but somehow all of that falls into the background when she's in my arms.

"It isn't that bad, is it?"

"No." I press a kiss to the top of her head. I'd endure more to stay this close to her.

She takes the soap and works up a lather, running it over my body. I interrupt her periodically to kiss her. She bites my lower lip enough to sting and pull me back. She thinks she's distracting me from kissing her, but she's just winding me up again. A few more minutes of this, and I'm pressing her against the wall of the shower.

I need her. Again. It's impossible, and yet she's proven that anything is possible with her. I don't recognize myself or my irrational physical responses. I'm ready to shove my cock into her again until she screams. Then she grasps my arms again.

"Wait."

I freeze. Concern stops my single-minded agenda in its tracks. But her eyes are soft and glimmering with a touch of mischief.

"You've already had me once," she says lightly.

"I want you more than once. I want to lose count. I have no idea when it'll ever be enough, Madison." I guide my hand between her thighs and stroke between her folds, barely grazing her clit.

"I feel the same way. But I can't get lost between the sheets with you again this fast. We should talk. We should go out."

My muscles tighten. "Out?"

As if sensing my impending anxiety, she slides her body against mine and presses a wet kiss to my neck, lathing her tongue over the same place. I slip two fingers into her pussy in reply. She moans, but a small smile curls her lips.

"Come on, Luke. Let's venture out. Just an hour. You and me. I want to discover a little bit of this place with you."

I reach deeper, hoping I can coax out an orgasm before she can take me on this plan that has me freaking out already.

"You can make me come again, but I'll ask you the same thing afterwards."

I exhale and rest my head against the shower wall beside her. She is such a pain in the ass. And I should be freaking out a little more than I am. What the hell.

My first mistake was letting her drive. I haven't needed to in so long, I figured why add to the discomforts of the day. But Madison has no idea where she's going, and as a result is driving like a nut. Too fast, too slow, and then over the curb that leads to downtown Avalon.

Main Street is dead. A few flashing signs and a collection of cars that sit outside Mo's Hole in the Wall.

"This place looks good," she says with far too much enthusiasm.

I cringe and briefly consider taking the wheel. "I'm not going to a bar with you."

She ignores me, parks, and then turns toward me. "Listen, you put me on this crazy roller coaster. You owe me this."

I flinch back. "You started this 'roller coaster' actually. Barging into my cabin uninvited, remember?"

"Well you kept me there, and then you seduced me. Repeatedly."

I throw my hands up. "What was I supposed to do?"

"And then you kicked me out, after getting me completely addicted to...basically everything about you. You pushed me out of my comfort zone."

I press my lips together and stare at her a second too long. "And let me guess. You're pushing me out of mine."

"Yes," she replies without hesitation.

She smiles, and I hate that I know I'm going to give in no matter what. I hope she knows how this goes against everything I want.

"Walking down the mountain was out of my comfort zone, Maddy. I don't like coming into town. It's not something you'll probably ever understand."

Her smile fades and she reaches across the center console to touch my arm. "I'm with you."

"I don't need protection."

She leans over and brushes her lips across mine. "Not with me, you don't. I like how it feels when you come in me."

She strokes her tongue into my mouth, and all my thoughts turn to sex. Little fucking minx is pressing all my buttons to get what she wants. Fine. I'll go to this goddamn dive bar, and then I am going back to the retreat and fucking her six ways from Sunday. I'll have earned it.

"Let's go, before I bend you over the car."

She giggles and is out of the car before I can even think about getting my hard-on under control. I take a few deep breaths and reach for the door handle. I pause a second and watch her wait for me on the sidewalk. She bounces in place. Something about her giddiness warms my heart and works against all the instincts that are shouting at me to run back up the mountain.

CHAPTER TEN

MADISON

I sweep my thumb across the back of his, our hands clasped tightly together as we walk into Mo's. "It'll be okay, Luke. Come on," I whisper when he hesitates.

Shit, this is bad. Maybe I shouldn't have pushed him to come here. My attempt to remind him of all the good things he's missing out on by hiding away in his cabin may have been too selfish.

His eyes scan the crowded room. Only a few steps inside the bar and his grip on my hand tightens.

"You okay?"

"Yeah."

"We can go." I second guess my idiotic idea until he smiles, and the knot that formed in my stomach starts to unfurl.

He leans forward, brushing his lips tenderly against mine. "I'm fine, Madison."

My hand squeezes his tightly and I nod slowly, unsure if he means it. "Okay," I whisper against his lips. Gazing into his deep blue eyes, I finally let myself relax.

Luke leads me through the crowd like he's done it a million

times, and motions for me to slide in the booth first. When he sits next to me, he places his warm, strong hand on top of my knee.

I relax into his hard, muscular side and rest my head on his shoulder. "You hungry?"

"I could eat, but I'd rather eat you." He smirks.

The playful flirting turns me on, but then again, everything about Luke does.

"That can be arranged," I tease and slowly lick my lips, drawing his gaze to my mouth.

"Madison." His eyes darken. "I'm hanging on by a thread here. I want nothing more than to take you somewhere and bury my face between your soft thighs. So be a good girl."

The guilt I had been feeling is quickly wiped away when his hand slides up my thigh and his pinky finger brushes against my panty line underneath my skintight pants.

"We can leave if you want." My voice is husky, overcome by lust. I never stand a chance with Luke. Just a simple touch sends me into overdrive.

"Hi, I'm Maureen. What can I get you to drink?" The waitress interrupts our moment.

She's tapping her pen against a small pad of paper and staring at Luke.

"I'll take a Pepsi, please," I say, trying to get her attention away from Luke. When he doesn't answer her, I give him a little nudge with my shoulder.

"Water." He keeps his gazed fixed on me.

"Do you two want menus?"

"Yes," I answer.

She studies him for a few seconds before finally walking away. I can tell her curiosity has nothing to do with the fact that he's new, because she didn't bother to size me up in the way she did him. Her fixation on him is something more.

"This is a bad idea," I whisper when she's out of ear range, that guilt creeping back in.

"It's fine. I'm used to the stares."

"You shouldn't have to be used to them, Luke." I scan the room and notice more than a few sets of eyes on us. "What's up everyone's ass in this place?" My heart aches for Luke and I want to smack myself for forcing him to come here.

Just when I'm about to tell him again that we can leave, he moves his hand from my knee around the back of the booth, resting it on my shoulder. "It's fine, Madison."

"It's not."

He presses his soft, warm lips to my forehead. "They've all seen me before, but I think they're more curious about the woman by my side."

"They're not looking at me."

"They're looking at us," he says, pulling me closer to his body. "They're wondering if I kidnapped you." A deep laugh trickles out of him.

I'm horrified that they would even think such a thing. "That's just ridiculous," I snarl.

The tiny crinkles near the corners of his eyes deepen when he smiles. "Well, I'm sure it's what they're thinking. How did *that man* find a woman?"

"Pepsi and a water," Maureen says, sliding them in front of us.

When neither of us look up, she clears her throat. "Anything to eat?"

"I'll take a cheeseburger and fries," I say. It's a safe bet. Shitholes like this always have them on the menu.

Keeping his gaze locked on mine and almost oblivious to Maureen's gawking, he tells her, "I'll have the same."

We sit in silence, curled together without any space between us as we wait. I'm dying to ask him about everything I found during my Internet search. But I can't figure out a way to do it without sounding like a stalker. Technically, I did stalk him, but it was only online and everything I found was public knowledge. My need to figure out Luke Dawson overtook my sanity. I knew it was wrong to invade his privacy in that way, but it didn't stop me.

Someone drops a plate behind us and it shatters into what sounds like a million little pieces. Luke jolts and tenses.

"It was just a plate." I place my hand on his leg, anchoring him to the now. "You're okay, Luke. I'm here." I keep my voice soft and soothing.

He blinks a few times before finally relaxing his death grip against my shoulder. "This is why I stay away from people."

Turning to him, I cup his face in my hands. "Is it too much for you? We can go if you—"

"No." He cuts me off, places his hands over mine, and returns my smile. "I'm okay. I want to spend time with you, even if it means I'm a little uncomfortable. Stop asking me if I want to leave. When I want to go, I'll go. End of story."

I search his face, but see nothing but truth in his eyes. "Yes, sir," I say, trying to lighten the mood. "So..." I purse my lips and try to figure out what to talk about. Luke and I haven't talked much even though we've spent a good amount of time with each other.

"So..." he repeats.

I roll my eyes. The man is impossible. "Tell me something about yourself. Something you haven't told anyone in years."

His thumb strokes the exposed skin on my shoulder before he answers. "I like cheeseburgers," he says with a slight smirk.

He thinks he's done, but I shake my head and forge on. "That doesn't count. Everybody likes cheeseburgers."

"Well." He pauses and continues to softly graze my skin.

"Give me something. Please."

"I was married before."

My head snaps backward with the news. "You were?"

"Yep."

"When?" There was nothing on his online profile that indicated that he was married or divorced. No mention of a woman at all. "Your choice or hers?" I blurt the question out before he has a chance to answer the first one.

"Hers. We divorced while I was deployed during my last tour." He shrugs like it's no big deal, but it's huge.

What type of cold-hearted bitch divorces her hero soldier husband while he's on the front lines and his life hangs in the balance?

I narrow my eyes at him. "What an asshole."

"Being the wife of a soldier isn't an easy life. Especially when I couldn't even tell her where I was or what I was doing every day. There were too many secrets for us to survive."

"It's still a bitch move, Luke."

He leans forward and kisses my forehead with so much tenderness I want to smack his ex-wife for breaking his heart. "We've both had shitty things happen to us, Madison."

My chest aches with the truthfulness of his words. I can't imagine what he lived through, having his heart broken, and so far away that there was nothing he could do.

When Jeremy broke me, I'd wanted to curl into a ball. The helplessness I felt eventually led me to the Avalon and to this moment sitting by Luke's side. But I didn't have to dodge bullets from an enemy, just the paparazzi trying to make a quick buck.

He's right though. We'd both had shitty deals. But I know one thing for sure. When I'm with Luke, nothing that happened before matters. Not Jeremy. Not his affair. Not even my personal life becoming front page news. The only thing that matters is Luke and the way he makes me feel.

LUKE

I can't tell if I see pity in her eyes or a realization that she isn't alone. When she told me about her ex, I didn't confess this part of my past. But I know what it's like to love someone and have them turn their back on you. When the divorce papers were delivered to me, I was shocked. No, that's an understatement. I was knocked off kilter. My wife had been my only reason for making it through each day. What reason would I have to live, to come back, without her waiting for me?

"I'm sorry." Madison stares up at me as she laces our fingers together. "I had no idea."

"It was a long time ago. I'm over it."

It had taken me a while, but I got over her. I moved on and found a new path, one that led me to my mountain. I didn't cloister myself away because of her, but I certainly couldn't handle civilization without her by my side. Looking back now, I wouldn't change a thing. Because all of that brought me to this place, this time, with Madison by my side.

"Two cheeseburgers," Maureen says, placing the plates in front of us with her eyes trained on me.

Madison glares at the waitress. "Is there something you need, Maureen? That's your name, right?"

Here we go. The whole time I worried about how I'd react to the people here, but I should've been worried about Madison. I've grown used to their stares, but this was new to her.

Maureen scrunches her nose and snarls. "No."

"Are you sure? Because every time you come over here you rudely stare at my boyfriend, and I'm trying to figure out why."

I glance up toward the ceiling and curse under my breath. This is going to be bad. My stomach's growling, the cheesy beefy goodness of the burger's calling to me, but I have a feeling I'm not going to get even a small taste.

Maureen rests her hands flat on the table top and her extra-large body casts a shadow over the booth. "I don't know who you think you are, missy. But your kind isn't welcome here."

"My kind?" Madison's eyebrows rise before she laughs loudly.

Maureen straightens and places her hands on her hips, making her already wide frame appear even bigger. "We don't take to strangers."

Madison crosses her arms over her chest and cocks her head. "Is that why you can't keep your eyes off Luke?"

Their voices get louder, drawing the attention of everyone

around us. A hush falls over the room as they turn to face us. Not me, but the two women on either side of me ready to go at it at any moment. The problem is, I'm going to have to step in before it gets out of hand.

"Ladies." I glance from Maureen to Madison. "Let's just forget this ever happened." I reach in my back pocket and grab a twenty, throwing it on the table. "We're just going to go."

Madison grabs my wrist as I start to stand. "Sit." Her tone is firm and completely sexy.

I drop back into the booth and grit my teeth. "You're not going to be the one that has to clean this mess up, sweetheart," I say with my jaw clenched and a fake smile on my face. "I don't feel like getting in a fight."

"Don't be so dramatic, dear," she tells me with a glare. "So, Maureen." She turns her attention back to the waitress, whose mouth is now hanging open as she watches our exchange. "What's with the face?"

Maureen narrows her eyes and starts to say something, but when a hand clamps down on her shoulder, she snaps her mouth shut.

"Problem over here, Reenie?" The guy beside her virtually comes out of nowhere.

"This girl." Maureen points her stubby little finger toward Madison and glowers. "She has no manners, Melvin."

Melvin looks at Madison before setting his sights on me. He's twice my width, but I'm sure there're muscles underneath his pot belly and man breasts. The old white tank top that barely covers his middle is covered in stains and he adds to them when he wipes his hands on his sides. "I think you need to take your piece of ass and burger to go," he says, pitching a thumb over his shoulder.

"Excuse me?" Madison pipes in.

I brace myself for the inevitable fistfight that's going to take place.

"We were minding our own business, getting ready to eat dinner, but Maureen here..." Madison's glare intensifies. "She's being rude, and I think she's the one that needs to leave."

Maureen laughs, revealing her teeth, or lack thereof, when her head tips back.

My hand tightens on Madison's knee. We're overstepping. This isn't LA. People around these parts tend to stick together, and we're the outsiders. "Stop," I tell her, my voice low and hushed so only she can hear.

Melvin joins in, laughing loudly and running his hand through his greasy hair before his expression becomes cold and angry. "Take your mouthy bitch and get the fuck out of here."

I'm on my feet, standing toe-to-toe with Melvin before he finishes the sentence. Every muscle in my body is tense, and my anger is about to bubble over. "You need to watch your mouth."

"I'm not sayin' nothing that isn't true. You should put a muzzle on her." Melvin glances around my shoulder and barks in Madison's direction.

The last few years I've been a patient man. I've let things slide off my back just to keep the peace, preferring to stay in the background and secluded in my own little world. But Melvin's statement gets under my skin.

My instincts kick in and I punch Melvin on the chin, snapping his jack backward. He staggers backward and tries to grab on to a chair for support. But he misses and wobbles. Eventually he finds his footing and starts heading back in my direction with his fist clenched tightly.

But before he can throw a punch, another guy steps in front of me and swings. I weave backward and to the side before I launch an even more devastating blow than the one that connected with Melvin's face. The new guy, who I suppose is Melvin's friend, falters for a moment before coming back for more.

Madison's pleading for me to stop, but her voice is faint as she tugs on my arm. I shake her off, pushing her lightly back toward the relative safety of the booth.

My training has kicked in, my focus narrows on my targets, and I ready myself to use any means necessary to get out safely with Madison at my side. The two men coming after me—and the country boy onlookers—are no match for my skills. I make quick work of the two, laying them out on the floor with a few more blows.

When I turn toward Madison, her lips are parted and she's clutching her chest.

"Come on." I hold my bruised hand out for her to take.

I'm done with this place. Done with the town that's supposed to be part of my home. My welcome has worn out, and before the other shitkickers want to try and take me down too.

Madison slides her hand into mine and tucks herself under my arm, resting her hand on my stomach. Neither of us say anything until we make it outside.

"Give me the keys." She pauses just outside the truck and holds out her hand.

I shake my head and reach into my pocket. "I'm driving. Get your ass in the truck, Madison." I open the door and motion for her to get in without any more lip.

I help her inside the cab, and she grabs my face.

"Luke. I want you."

"Madison," I say, righting her in the seat. "Not now." As I walk around, making my way to the driver's side, I wonder how I let this woman into my world. Nothing has made sense since I caught her at the springs. Everything really went out of whack the moment she showed up at my door. I slide into the seat and turn on the engine. "It's going to be a long ride home."

She licks her lips and her gaze travels up the length of my body. "The Avalon is closer." She gives me a quick and playful wink.

"The Avalon it is," I tell her before closing the door.

I drive us straight to the Avalon with her body practically entangled around mine the entire way. We barely make it into the room before we're undressing, throwing our clothes on the ground. I follow her to the bed and fall on top of her.

Even though the evening was a shit show, I end up exactly where I want to be—with Madison underneath me.

CHAPTER ELEVEN

LUKE

"Oh God. Oh God!" Madison digs her fingernails into the sheets on either side of her.

My face is buried between her thighs, and I'm taking my sweet time. She's already come once. I'm bringing her there slowly on round two.

She drags her heel up the middle of my back to urge me on, but nothing's going to make me push her over the edge before I'm good and goddamn ready to.

"I want to come, Luke. Don't make me wait..."

"I'll make you wait as long as I want to. And you'll like it," I murmur against her wet flesh. I secure her legs, holding them firmly apart so I can lap up her creamy arousal as she gives it to me. I'm faintly hungry, but I'd been telling the truth before. I'd rather eat her. And even though my cock wants to be reunited with her delicious pussy, I'm appreciating this appetizer before the entree.

I pride myself on my patience. Life's too precious to rush through it. Years can fly by and might amount to nothing. An experience worth having is one worth fully experiencing. I am not wishing this away... I am not wishing her away.

Nothing about my time with Madison makes me think she feels the same way. She's always rushing. Running head first into situations she hasn't thought through. From barging into my cabin last week to mouthing off to the waitress an hour ago. She's all passion and no goddamn sense.

I don't want fly-by-night. And I don't want her spending time with me for the wrong reasons. I wasted years with someone who'd moved on too quickly with someone else. I don't blame my ex completely for our failed marriage, but I'd learned a powerful lesson about relying too much on the wrong people. I never want to find myself in that position again.

A low moan crawls past Madison's throat and she arches off the bed, her body forming a tense bow. She's right there. Right there...

I pull my mouth off and flick her clitoris with my index finger... hard.

"Ahhh!" She screams and lifts her head to glare down at me. "What the hell are you doing to me?"

I lick my lips and smile. I glide the pads of my wet fingertips over her swollen bud. Back and forth, soft and steady. Her glare melts into an expression of beautiful agony. Her lips fall open and her head falls back. Her long dark hair pools on the bedspread. Shadows play off her body, the incredible curves of her breasts, and the sheen of sweat that matches her scorching skin.

"Please..." She's trembling. Shudders take over her body every time I add the faintest pressure.

I want to make her wait. I'm tempted to fucking torture her right now. But I have needs too, and I've been patient long enough.

I rise to my feet and haul her roughly to the edge of the bed. Her eyes are wide as I fold her calves around my waist.

"Put me in that position again, Madison...and I'll keep you hanging for hours. Do you hear me?"

Her glare starts to return, but she's too hazy with lust to give it much force. I fist my cock and stroke firmly. I'm so fucking ready to be inside her. I know she wants it too. Her gaze fixes there and she lifts her hips infinitesimally.

"Do you hear me?" I lift an eyebrow and drag the tip of my aching cock over her clit and down through her drenched folds until I'm exactly where I need to be.

Another whimper escapes her lips, but she doesn't tell me what I want to hear. Without warning, I shove into her with one hard thrust.

"Yesss!"

That one word becomes long and desperate and fills the room. Whether it's all rapture or some small part acknowledgment of her fuck up, I can't be sure, but her scream gets under my skin and mingles with my insane desire for her. Fuck me, she was made for me. The glorious pressure of her cunt gloving my cock is making me dizzy already.

My patience has expired. I begin to fuck her. Harder than I usually do. Maybe because I've still got adrenaline spiking my blood. Maybe because I'm unsettled by everything about tonight. Whatever the reason, we're barreling toward release, hard and fast...together. I give her clit one last bit of attention, and she crushes down on me with a thready cry. Then I'm emptying everything that I am into her...

MADISON

I'm vaguely aware of the bathroom vent humming in the background. The shower turning on and then off. The silence becomes loud when Luke's footsteps end inside the bedroom. I'm on cloud nine, but the heat of my orgasm eventually fades and I grab a handful of sheet to cover myself with. I lift my head and see Luke sitting on the chair by the desk. His lower body is wrapped in a white towel and his arms hang casually off the sides of the chair. His gaze is trained on me.

I blink a few times, trying to pull myself back to the land of the living. "Is everything okay?"

He's silent, and every second that goes by alarms me. He brings one hand to his face and absently rubs the rough hair on his cheek. It's a tick. He does it when he's pensive. Thinking about something and doesn't know I'm watching him.

"I honestly don't know," he says quietly.

I sit up and bring the sheet tighter around my torso. "Talk to me."

"I am talking to you."

I roll my eyes. "Jesus—"

"Don't give me shit, Maddy. We left here in the first place so we could talk. I get halfway through a confession about my failed marriage and you're picking a fight. And getting off on it."

I open my mouth but I'm struggling to find the right words. He's literally fucked my brains out. Great.

Then he's on his feet and coming toward me. Crawling up the bed, he pressures me to my back again. He's totally throwing me off, but he prevents me from saying anything when he kisses me.

He kisses me like we haven't spent the past couple hours feasting on each other. He kisses me like in the few minutes he was sitting in that chair, he missed me.

When he pulls back, I search his gaze breathlessly. Those blue eyes are two oceans full of memories and thoughts I know too little about. I'm about to beg him to open up to me when he speaks again.

"I'm falling in love with you, Madison."

My mouth hangs open dumbly. My heart's thundering now, reverberating in my ears. The intensity in his gaze never wavers.

"I love your body. Every beautiful inch of it. I love the way you try to protect me, even though I have no need for it. I love that you try to do things your own way, even when it's idiotic and ill-timed."

I frown and think about arguing, but he brushes his thumb across my lips, distracting me with his tenderness again.

"I can't help how I feel now. So when you ask me if I'm okay, I'm telling you I don't really know. I'm not sure what this means or what's really going on between us. All I know is I want to be more than a man who can get you wet because he can lay a few guys out."

"No! That's not..."

I pressure his shoulder and he rolls to his side. I roll to mine so we can face each other with a little more equality. But I'm feeling off kilter and completely awful as his words filter through me a few more times. He loves me...and he thinks I'm a total whore.

I close my eyes with a sigh. "Luke, everything about you arouses me. Watching you build a fire. Chop wood. Warm up soup in a pathetic little pot for me. You knocking on my door gets me wet, for God's sake. Trust me, there is no end to the things that do."

He's quiet, and I scramble for more words... Hopefully the right ones.

"I'm sorry I put you in that position. I had no idea those people were going to act like barbarians."

"I'm the one who put my fist to their faces, remember?"

"And they deserved it!" I poke a finger at his strong chest, reliving the moment with a little too much enthusiasm. I wanted to see justice doled out on those assholes. "Did it occur to you that maybe they needed to learn a lesson? Maybe next time they see you they'll have some more respect."

Luke shrugs. "Or they'll bring a search party up the mountain for me."

"They wouldn't." My eyes go wide despite my doubts.

A reassuring smile curves the corners of his lips. "Don't worry. I don't think a big boy like Melvin's going to make it too far up the mountain. And if he did, he'd be too winded to pose much of a threat. But I'm guessing I won't be getting any dinner invites next time I'm in town for supplies."

My lips tighten, and in that moment, I'm overwhelmed with how unfair Luke's existence is. He may be content with it, but the fact that experiences beyond his control drove him up there and now the people in this know-nothing town keep him there is more than I can accept.

"You deserve more than this," I say softly.

His expression is calm and unchanged. "What would you have me do? I'm not like you. I'm not cut out for city life. Small towns are always going to pose their own challenges. It's something I came to terms with a long time ago."

I exhale a sigh. "You really love me?"

He lifts his hand to my face and strokes his thumb across my cheekbone. "Yeah. I really do."

I'm not caught up over how quickly feelings have formed between us. What's got the words knotted in my throat is the fact that I've never said them to anyone but Jeremy. I always meant it, even when I said it in passing, even at the bitter end. He'd always have a place in my heart...but I was a long way from being *in love* with my ex-husband. That chapter had long closed. He was my past.

Was Luke Dawson my future?

I lean in and kiss him softly. "I'm falling for you too," I whisper against his lips. "As scary as it is, I can't help how you've made me feel. It's not just the way you make me forget my own name. No one's ever made me feel so safe, so...cared for. And I've given you no reason to—"

"Madison, stop with that. You deserve love. You deserve a real man. I don't know who your ex is, but I know he's a fucking idiot to let you go. I'm glad as hell he did though." He sifts his fingers through my hair, massaging my scalp as he does. "Because I haven't been this happy in a long time. And that's all you, sweetheart."

I release a heavy sigh and close my eyes. This man... God, his words and his body, and the way he's managed to rescue my heart from the depth of my misery and pull it into the warmth of his love. What did I ever do to deserve him? Even as I admit all of this to myself, the reality of my life outside of Avalon creeps in. I thought this was a fling, but it's rapidly becoming more. The thought of walking away from Luke in a few weeks is now unbearable.

"How are we going to make this work?"

He blinks and shakes his head slightly. "I have no idea."

"I'm here for three more weeks."

"And then?"

I take my lower lip between my teeth and chew it as my thoughts whirl around the possibilities. "We'll have to figure it out somehow. Our lifestyles are admittedly really far apart. I say we spend the next few weeks trying to find some middle ground."

He lifts an eyebrow. "Middle ground?"

I should be freaking out that we'll never find a way to be together, but something about this moment heartens me. I've been thinking about life's cup as half empty for so long, but somehow I have faith that we'll find a way to fill each other up and be together. Either that or I'm totally unwilling to contemplate the alternative—us walking away from each other in a few weeks.

"You love your place on the mountain."

"It's home," he answers softly.

"And my home is in LA."

"I'd prefer hours of torture over that life."

I nod quickly, because I can no more imagine him happy there than me being permanently content with a life in his log hut.

I trace my fingertips over his soft lips and trail them down across his beard. My beautiful rugged mountain man. "That's why we need to find a middle ground. Kind of like this place... Avalon. It's not your oasis on the mountain, and it's not in town with all those ignorant assholes. But it's someplace we can both be. We'll both have to step out of the lifestyles that make us comfortable, test our boundaries, and find that place where we can both be happy, together."

"Where would that be?"

I shake my head. "I have no idea. But I'm not walking away from you, so I'm committed to figuring it out."

He's silent for a moment. His blue eyes are intense, flickering mirrors of swirling emotion. We're making big promises. We're baring souls. I'm scared and enlivened all at once.

"Okay," he finally says. "We'll figure it out. I'll... I'll do the best I can."

I smile, and my heart swells with happiness and hope. I haven't felt like this since—I can't remember when my soul felt so alive. I launch forward to wrap my arms around Luke, my lover, my love...

CHAPTER TWELVE

LUKE

"I have an idea," Madison says in a voice that tells me I'm not going to like what comes out of her mouth next.

We've been holed up in the cabin for two days, enjoying each other without interruption after spending a night at the Avalon. I know it's going to come to an end, because she's going stir crazy. I can see it in her eyes even though she hasn't said the words. I'm content and probably the happiest I've been in years. I'm lying to myself though. I know we can't stay like this forever.

"Need my cock again?" I glance down at her nakedness. She's curled into my side on the couch as we watch the fire crackling and hissing in the fireplace.

She smirks and her eyes sparkle, reflecting the flickering flames of the fire. "Yes, but that's not it." She straddles me, placing her knees on either side of my legs.

"If it doesn't involve my cock, I don't want to hear it." I roll my hips, pushing my erection into her middle. There are perks to being naked all the time. Easy access to her body being the biggest.

"Luke." She makes a very serious face, leaning forward enough to make my cock twitch with appreciation. "Stop thinking about my pussy for two seconds."

Gripping her hips roughly, I still her movement. "Stop grinding against me, and I'll stop thinking about it, sweetheart."

She tips her head back and giggles softly for a moment. I lift up and drag my lips against her neck.

"Stop." She plants her hands against my chest and pushes me backward. "So..." She pauses with a mischievous smirk. "I thought we could do something different today."

"Different?"

She nods slowly, moves her hand to my neck, and runs her hands through my beard. "You know what I do for a living, right?"

It takes everything in me not to groan. "Yeah."

"Well, how about I give this beard a trim." She gives me a soft smile as her fingers rake through my hair. "And then maybe..." Her smile turns into a hesitant grimace. "Maybe we can cut your hair."

I suck my lip into my mouth, chewing on the pieces of my beard that have grown over. It's been a long time since I've cleaned it up. There was no need to when it was only me. "I'll let you trim my beard, but it's a no go on the hair, Madison."

"Hmm." She rubs her chin slowly as she studies me. "Can I shave the beard off? I'm dying to know what you look like underneath all that hair."

"You can *trim* it. If you want more than that, you have to give a little."

"Can we put the hair back on the table?" She twists her lips to the side, challenging me.

I sigh and decide to give her some hope, depending on how

things turn out. "Fine. But I get to decide when, where, and how much."

"I'll do anything." She bounces up and down right on my aching dick.

I growl and dip my hips so the tip of my dick presses against her wet heat. "Right now, I want to slide into that sweet pussy." I slide my hand up her back, fisting her hair in my hands. Our gazes lock and her laughter dies. I tip her head back and lean forward, running my lips down her neck. "And fuck you until you pass out."

"Oh." She digs her fingernails into my bare shoulders when I bite down on the curve of her neck.

She raises and brings herself down on my length. Shivers rake across my body and I close my mouth around her nipple, moaning against her skin as her insides clamp down against me. I can't even remember how many times we've fucked, but each time it's like it's the first time.

With one hand on her hip and the other still in her hair, I move her body up and back down, meeting each downward stroke with a roll of my hips. Within minutes, she's taking control and slamming her body down my shaft, grinding her clit before she peels herself back and repeats the movement. I slide my hand to her ass and bring it down hard against her tender flesh.

She bucks and her eyes widen, but she doesn't skip a beat.

"Fuck me, Madison. I want to feel you come on my cock." I soothe the battered flesh with my palm. When her body starts to shake with an impending orgasm, I smack her ass again, causing my own hand to sting in the most pleasurable way.

Her eyes blaze with lust. "Do it again and see what happens," she says in a deep, wanton voice.

My interest is piqued, and I can't resist the urge to slap her ass again. But when I do, she does something I don't expect—she smacks my face. I'm taken aback by the assault. No one's ever hit me while they were fucking me, but it was...fucking hot.

I run my tongue along my lip as it starts to swell and ache, and gaze at her. Just when I think I know her, she does something that throws me for a loop.

"Too much?" She hovers over me with just the tip of my cock inside her.

I pull her down, crushing my mouth to her as an answer. I'm more turned on than I was before. But I need more. The position doesn't give me the leverage and angle I want. Standing with her in my arms and my cock buried deep inside her, I place her back against the couch and thrust into her. The strokes are punishing, deep, and fast. I slide my hand up her back and curl my fingers around her shoulder, pulling her toward me with each blow.

Using my upper body, I push her legs forward, allowing me to go deeper and stroke her G-spot. Her muscles strain and her thighs press against my arms as her body starts to shake underneath me. She's moaning my name and gasping for air. But I batter her pussy harder and drive her over the edge. I follow, moaning and lost in an orgasmic haze with her. I collapse on top of her, pressing her into the cushion with my weight as I gasp for air, trying to fill my empty lungs.

"I'm sorry," she whispers in my ear as I start to come to.

I suck in a breath and exhale. "For what?"

"I didn't mean to hit you, but..."

I pull back and stare down into her beautiful, soft eyes. "It was fucking hot, Madison."

She smiles and bites her bottom lip. "I kinda liked it."

I roll my body onto the floor, taking her with me, and burst into laughter. "I love you."

She rubs her nose against mine. Pressing her tits against my chest, she smiles down at me. "I love you too, Luke." She shimmies down my body and tucks her head under my chin, resting it on my chest. "So about that promise."

MADISON

I hold my breath. *Please give in.* The man hasn't budged about much, but I'm dying to find out what's underneath the caveman beard. I'll admit he's sexy as hell with it, but I know there's something more beautiful behind the mass of hair that covers his face and neck. The cutout near his mouth shows a hint of his full lips. I've felt them. I know they're there, just hidden behind the endless layers of facial hair that have started to overtake them.

He sighs. "You really want to do this?"

I know it's a hard thing for him to agree to because it means change. From what I've seen, he hasn't changed anything in years.

"I do." I kiss him softly. "I want to kiss your lips without your hair in the way."

"You make it sound good." He looks up at me with the softest blue eyes and tucks an errant strand of hair behind my ear. "I'll let you, but..." His voice trails off and he smirks.

"What?" I'm scared to hear the rest of the sentence.

"I'm going to reserve my payback for a later date. I have something in mind, but I want it to be a surprise."

"If it's anal, you can keep the hair." I laugh loudly which earns me another swat on my ass.

"If it's anal I want, I don't need to make a deal to get it."

I purse my lips and pretend that what he's saying isn't true, but we both know it is. "Ya think?"

He rolls, pinning me under him on the fuzzy bearskin rug in front of the fire. "I know," he says in a deep edgy voice that steals my breath.

"Yeah," I whisper, not trusting myself to speak any louder. The thought of him violating me in that way sends tiny shockwaves throughout my body.

"Madison," he murmurs against my lips and presses his hardened length against my core. "If you want to trim my beard, you better do it now before I fuck you again."

I press my hand against his chest, pushing him off me and climbing to my feet before he can sink into me again.

As I wobble to the bathroom, the evidence of our earlier sexual escapade trails down my thigh. I clean myself up and grab the scissors from under the sink before practically skipping back to the living room because I'm overflowing with excitement.

He's lying on his back with his hands tucked under his head and staring up at the ceiling when I straddle him. The fire creates shadows across his muscles, the caverns the deepest black. My mouth waters and my fingers itch to touch him again. I gaze down at him and clear my mind, focusing on the task at hand.

My willpower almost slips when his hands slide up my legs and come to rest on my hips.

"You sure?" My voice cracks when his fingertips dig deliciously into my flesh.

"Completely." Unlike mine, his tone is firm and steady.

I hold the tools up, jiggling them back and forth over him. "I need better light to not do a hack job on you. Sit in the chair." I extract myself off his body and instantly miss his warmth.

I stand in awe as he rolls to his stomach and does a push-up before climbing to his feet. My mouth falls open as I gawk at his body. Every muscle ripples when he moves. Fuck. The man seriously doesn't have an ounce of body fat anywhere.

He settles into the chair and leans back, placing his hands on the armrests. "Climb on." He smirks seductively.

Standing in front of him completely naked without so much as a care about my body, I place one hand on my hip and cock my head. "A few rules first."

He groans and rolls his eyes. "I'll keep my hands to myself," he replies as if he read my mind.

I step forward but don't straddle him yet. I don't trust myself to not give in if he decides to not play fair. "Keep *everything* to yourself."

"My hands won't move." He drops his gaze to the armrest. "Scout's honor."

I only hesitate for a moment, before sliding against his thick legs. I instantly regret the rules because I miss his touch. My knees dig into the cushion as I reach over to the end table, set down the scissors, and pull the oil lamp closer.

He watches me as I take in his beauty, studying his every feature. In the light, he looks gentle and kind, especially his usually dark, intense blue eyes. Working slowly, I start with his neck. I cut away the bristle that covers his Adam's apple and work my way up.

Once the skin on his neck is visible, I move the clippers toward his jawline and pull away to make sure I don't take too much.

Once his beard is shorter and less bushy, I set down the clippers and grab the scissors. I slide my index finger across his top lip, feeling every strand prickle my fingertip. His lips move under my touch as he smiles and our eyes connect.

He's been completely still and silent during the process. Our eyes have found each other a few times, but his stare has been constant. I've wondered more than once what he's thinking, but I don't dare ask. I don't want anything to sidetrack me before the job is done.

"You okay?"

"Yeah." He drags his tongue across his bottom lip in a teasing manner. "Are you?"

I narrow my eyes at him and won't let him derail me. "I'm fine."

"How do I look?"

He starts to move his hand toward his face, but I swat it away.

"Ah. Ah. Ah. No moving," I remind him with a playful smile as I hold the scissors near his lips. "We wouldn't want my hand to slip and for you to get cut."

He laughs softly. "If you injure my lips, it won't stop me from eating your beautiful pussy."

My hand trembles as his words ignite a fire inside me. I take two deep, calming breaths before starting to cut the wayward hairs that hang over his lips. When I'm done I sit back and look over my handiwork. Behind his whiskers are fuller, lusher lips than I ever imagined. Luke, the rugged mountain man, now looks like he could grace the cover of a magazine.

MEREDITH WILD & CHELLE BLISS

"Done?"

My gaze lingers on his mouth, and I watch the way his lips move when he speaks. Unable to wait another minute to feel them against me, I lean forward and press my mouth against his. I lose myself in the softness of his skin as he pushes his tongue deeper and demands more than a gentle kiss.

My grip loosens on the scissors and they fall to the floor next to the armchair. I push my chest against his. Tangling my fingers in his long hair, I snake my arms around his neck.

I never want this to end.

CHAPTER THIRTEEN

MADISON

I wake to the sounds of birds singing outside the window. I roll over and pull Luke's worn quilt around my naked body. Blinking my eyes open, I only see an empty cabin and a bright spring day pouring sunshine through the windows.

Luke must be doing some work outside. He teasingly reminds me I'm the one on vacation, while his existence here requires daily effort. I get it, and I respect it. But there's no way I could live this way day after day. I've been off the grid for a couple weeks, and I've loved it. I feel like I'm myself again, without the hectic life and convoluted relationships that brought me low. But I recognize that I'm getting restless. Unlike Luke, I don't have a purpose here. Unless being Luke's twenty-four-seven lover counts as a purpose, which I'm completely fine with.

Still, I can't help but wonder what's going on in the real world. I'd texted all my friends before I left that I wouldn't be in touch much, and while a few have checked in, for the most part, the people in my LA world have been quiet. I stretch, and with the quilt still around me, I get up to grab my phone from my bag and make myself a cup of coffee. There's already a pot warmed up for me, and I smile at Luke's unfailing thoughtfulness.

I settle into the chair we fucked on last night and power on my phone. Who knew trimming a man's beard would be so erotic? There was something oddly intimate about the act. His trust in me, and then seeing a different side of him physically had driven me wild. As the days go by, the more intense our lovemaking becomes. I'm seeing shades of Luke he never showed me before.

My thoughts float from memory to memory, each one arousing me more and making me wonder where the hell Luke is. Then my messages start to load and my heart stops when I see one from Jeremy.

I'm in Avalon. Tried calling you. Where are you? I need to talk to you.

A dozen more messages come in, some from him trying to get in touch with me, others from some mutual friends asking me if I'd heard about his mom. Good God, what happened?

I text Jeremy back, confirming he's in Avalon. He replies just as Luke walks in. He's wearing a white T-shirt and jeans, looking perfectly and effortlessly gorgeous as usual.

"Hey, beautiful." Smiling broadly, he comes toward me, leans down, and kisses me sweetly. "I brought you some blueberries for breakfast. And these." He puts a small bouquet of tiny pink flowers bound by a thin green leaf into my hands.

"They're beautiful, thank you."

His eyes soften as he watches me. Then he straightens and moves toward the kitchen, pulling out the canister where he stores his oatmeal.

"I hope you're hungry."

I am, but I have to figure out what's going on with Jeremy and his mother. "I have to go down to Avalon."

He turns with a frown. "Why?"

I draw in a deep breath, because suddenly the prospect of telling him that my ex-husband is in town is a little terrifying. Worlds are colliding in a way I wasn't expecting. Nothing about this trip was expected though.

"Jeremy is here," I say simply.

He turns to face me completely and braces his hands on the wooden counter behind him. "Your ex?"

I nod. "Something's going on with his mom. It sounds like it's an emergency."

"How does he know you're here?"

I hesitate and think about that, because I hadn't told him. We haven't exactly been on speaking terms for a while. "He must have found out from a mutual friend. I can't imagine he'd come all this way if it wasn't important."

He's silent, turns back to the counter, and continues fixing breakfast.

"Are you okay?"

"I'm fine," he mutters. "I'll walk you down after breakfast."

I stare down into my cooling coffee. "I'm not sure if that's a good idea."

"What, are you afraid I'm going to kick his ass?" There's humor in his voice, but there's something else. Something serious and worrisome.

I chuckle softly, but a little part of me is concerned he'll get protective and lash out at Jeremy. Because Jeremy is a superficial prick. He'll never understand a man like Luke. And knowing what I do about Luke, he'll instantly hate my ex, perhaps to the point of violence. If there's a real emergency, I don't want to complicate it with unnecessary relationship drama.

"I appreciate you offering to take me, but I think it's better if I go by myself. If something's really wrong, it's going to be uncomfortable explaining…"

He turns to me, his expression hard, a far cry from the one he walked in with. "Explaining what? Me?"

I take in another deep breath, because I'm pretty sure I'm screwed with this conversation either way.

"Luke, we just got a divorce."

"And he's moved on, right?" His lips are tight.

"Yes, but—"

"Then what's the problem?"

I sigh and walk to the bed where my clothes are. I dress swiftly, because I can't deal with where this conversation is going. I still have to get my ass down the mountain and deal with Jeremy. I can't get into it with Luke right now.

I'm dressed and have my bag ready when Luke's arm comes around my waist, turning me toward him. I suck in a breath when his mouth is an inch from mine.

"Madison…" His lips part but no words form for a few seconds. "I love you."

Why can't I ever get used to those words out of his mouth? I'm struck with the gravity of the sentiment every time. My heart twists. I want to consume and be consumed with the love that's radiating through me.

"I love you too, Luke. More than you can possibly understand. Believe me."

I wrap my arms around him and kiss him gently, teasing the tip of my tongue along his lower lip. The one kiss turns into more and has our hands roaming, my heart racing, and a hundred memories of rapture flying through my mind. But, we can't do this right now.

"Luke...we can't. I need to go figure out what's going on."

He's quiet, but his caresses slow.

"You know I want to stay," I whisper.

"If you're not back by sunset, I'll come down to you."

I nod. "Okay. I hope I'm not that long."

We pull ourselves from another heated kiss, and after he insists on taking me a few more times, I get on my way, alone. A few feet from the cabin, I can't ignore the sense of doom that creeps in around my heart as I'm walking away from him.

I spot Jeremy's slick black Beamer next to mine immediately. Our matching luxury vehicles used to be cute, but I can't wait to trade mine in. I shove that thought away and remind myself that something's gone wrong. He didn't come here to hear me catalogue all the ways I'd grown to loathe him.

I check my room, but it's empty, so I head into the main building. I spot him at the front desk chatting with Indigo. No, he's flirting. He's got his fuck-me eyes going, but Indigo only laughs nervously and avoids his roaming gaze. God, he's such a douchebag.

Keep it together.

"Jeremy," I say loudly, hoping I sound as emotionally detached as I want to be.

He turns with a practiced smile, which fades a bit as he sizes me up. "Wow."

I frown and cross my arms defensively. "What?"

He laughs and shakes his head. "Nothing, you just look... I don't know, different."

I tuck my hair behind my ear and feel heat rushing to my cheeks. I can't imagine how I must look. I can't imagine it because Luke doesn't keep mirrors all around his one-room cabin. I haven't worn makeup in weeks. Hell, I've scarcely worn clothes.

"Well, I'm not working or networking or socializing here. It's a retreat. It's not about how you look." There's nothing emotionally detached about my tone. I'm defensive and snappy and I want to rip Jeremy's face off thirty seconds into our conversation.

"No, I get it. That's not really what I meant." He sighs and all the humor has fled his features. "Listen, I'm sorry to bother you here. I'm sure I'm the last person you want to see."

"I got your text. What's going on with Susan?"

He shoots a quick glance to Indigo, who's listening to every word, and then back to me. "Is there any place to get a coffee around here? I left at the crack of dawn and could use a pick-me-up."

"Café is that way, all the way at the end of the hallway," Indigo says, pointing us in the right direction.

I lead the way, noting amenities the retreat offers that I'd never bothered to notice before, including a little store and a beautiful meditation room that I'll never use—because these people scare the hell out of me for some reason, and because I'd rather be in Luke's bed than anywhere else. That's my Zen place.

Together, Jeremy and I venture into the little café, order coffees, and take a seat by a window that offers a perfect view of the trail that leads up the mountain.

Great. I groan inwardly, because I already miss Luke. I miss our oasis in the mountains and the perfect simplicity that we've enjoyed for days on end. Despite all that, I shift my focus back to Jeremy and the issue at hand.

"So what's going on? Your text really worried me."

For the first time in a long time, I really look closely at him. Does he look different because we're divorced and I'm seeing him in a new light? I can't be sure, but worry lines etch his forehead and the skin around his eyes. His features seem sharper, less boyish. He lifts his gaze to mine, and suddenly I'm worried that something really has gone horribly wrong.

"She went into the hospital for walking pneumonia last week. She was really weak so they kept her. She had other symptoms though so they ran some tests. They think she's got some sort of blood poisoning. She's septic, and..." Tears glimmer in his eyes. "I don't know how much time she has, but she asked for you. My brother and dad are there, but when I couldn't reach you I just drove out here."

"Oh my God." I press my fingers to my lips, but I can't stop the tears from collecting and spilling down my cheeks. I launch out of my chair and he rises, pulling me into a tight embrace.

All the hate-filled words disappear. All I care about is getting back to LA to see his mother. She was a second mother to me, sometimes even more so. She was heartbroken when we split up, and I regretted the pain it put her through. More than that, I regretted how we'd never be in each other's lives the same way again. Family dinners, holidays... I'd never give her grandchildren.

"I can't believe this." I sob into his chest, because I'm so completely overwhelmed that she might die.

He holds me closer and strokes my back. "I know. I can't believe it. Honestly, I think I'm still kind of in shock. I'm not sure if it's really hit me yet. But if I'm being honest..."

He pulls back enough so I can look up at him. He strokes my cheek and smiles sadly. "The only silver lining from any of this is seeing you again. I was scared you wouldn't want to see me, but I can't tell you how good it feels to be with you again."

I swallow over the painful emotions and nod. I can't handle what he's saying. I can't process all of this so quickly.

"Madison."

I jump back at the sound of Luke's voice.

LUKE

If Madison was worried about me beating the shit out of her ex, she officially had good reason. I ball my fists tightly, and I feel an odd mix of sickness and blind rage as I approach them. She'd jumped back out of their embrace the second she heard my voice. I recognize the worry in her eyes as she looks from the man I'm ready to grind into sawdust back to me.

Before I can, Madison is coming toward me, positioning herself between us. "Luke, what are you doing here?"

I glare down at her, because I can't goddamn help myself. "I wanted to make sure you got down okay, so I followed behind. What are *you* doing here?"

Only then do I notice the tears in her eyes. Is this guy giving her shit? What the fuck is going on?

"Jeremy's mom is sick. They aren't sure how much time she has. I have to go home."

The nausea comes back with a force that threatens to knock me on my ass. I'm six feet seven, two hundred and fifty pounds, and this woman leaving my life has me ready to crack.

I shake my head. "Madison, no."

"I'll come back," she says in a pleading voice.

My chest hurts. Like a goddamn tree trunk landed on it. I can barely breathe. "When?"

Jeremy sidles up next to her, but is wise enough to keep a couple feet of distance between us.

"I'm Jeremy Cleary. I'm Madison's husband." He holds his hand out.

"Ex-husband," Madison clarifies quickly.

I take his hand and crush it as much as I can with a shake. "Luke Dawson. I've been fucking her since she got here."

"Luke!" She glares at me, her mouth gaping.

"What?" I shrug like she's being crazy, but I know it's all me right now.

Jeremy's face turns grim. "What a gentleman."

I take a step forward and he immediately takes one back. "Gentleman? You've got a lot of nerve."

"Stop it, right now." Madison takes my hand and leads us out of the café.

We get to the reception area and pass Indigo. Madison drops my hand, and I follow her toward the annex where her room is. She unlocks the door, and the second I shut it behind us I feel a measure of relief. To be alone, with her.

Even if she looks like she's ready to kill me. I can handle that.

"I'm sorry," I start, but I know she's not going to have it.

"You're sorry? First, you blatantly disobey my wish to meet with Jeremy alone."

"I was worried about you. That's never going to change, and I'm not apologizing for it."

"Okay, then you barge into the café like a fucking caveman ready to engage in a full blown pissing contest with my ex."

"Yes, and? What am I supposed to think when I see you in his arms? You're mine, and maybe I'm crazy, but I wanted him to know it."

She's quiet for a second, and I'm not sure why. She turns and starts packing her suitcase. "I know this wasn't the plan, but I have to go," she says quietly.

"She's *his* mother. Why do you need to go?"

She stops and comes toward me, fire in her eyes like I've never seen. "Because, Luke, you fucking idiot, I love her like a mother. And no matter what Jeremy did to me, she always stood by me. I love you, and I do not want to leave. But I *have* to go, because this might be my only chance."

I swallow hard because I'm so conflicted. I can't fix this. I can't protect her from the pain she feels, and nothing I can say will keep her with me. I consider the impossible...and make it possible.

"Let me come with you."

Her shoulders fall and her anger fades into sadness. "Luke, if circumstances were different..."

I nod before she can finish, but everything is locking up inside. Each wave of pain freezes into a wall around my heart. She's leaving, and though the reasons may be perfectly sound, it's ripping my heart out.

"Fine. Let me know if you need anything. You know where to find me."

I turn to go. I have to get the hell out of here. I take two long strides toward the door and am reaching for the knob when she grabs my arm. "Luke, wait. Don't go."

I turn, slam her against the door, and keep her there with the strength of my body. She sucks in a breath and slides her fingers roughly through my hair. I crash my lips onto hers and kiss her savagely. I do more than taste and suck. I'm fucking her mouth. I'm devouring her. I'm sucking and biting, delving into her the way I wish I was other places. And she's groaning the way she does when she can't wait a minute more to have me inside of her. In a matter of seconds, her pants are at her ankles and I'm struggling to get my cock into her fast enough.

I kiss her, pull her legs around me, and slide inside her with one hard shove.

She cries out, and I lose myself in the bliss of her body. I tell her I love her a dozen times. Maybe more. I've lost count. I should hold it back, to protect myself, but I can't. She's leaving, and a thousand things could keep her from coming back to me. This could be it.

She's coming, moaning and scratching her nails down my back. I want to come, but I don't want this to end. This can't be the end...

"Madison...baby...I can't." *I can't let you go...*

"Luke, I want you to come. Come inside me. Mark me. Make

me yours. I'm always going to be yours. Believe me. God, please, you have to believe me. I love you so much."

Her unfiltered words finish me. I thrust so hard, the wooden door at her back squeaks like it might not be able to hold up the force of me fucking her against it. Not with this kind of passion spiking my veins, not with this kind of desperation driving every move.

She screams and her next orgasm takes me under. I can barely keep my feet under me, but I manage as I fill her with my release.

I'm not sure how many minutes pass. Eventually her legs slip past my hips and her feet find the floor. I get my bearings enough to realize she's got tears in her eyes again. She's also got a huge hickey on her neck, and I probably left marks from fucking her so roughly. I wince with regret. The tree trunk is back on my chest with the force of all the emotions that I can't begin to sort through right now.

"I want to beg you not to go," I whisper.

She cradles my face in her palms and whispers back. "Come with me."

CHAPTER FOURTEEN

MADISON

There's an indescribable deafening silence when I drop my bags to the hardwood floor in my foyer and glance around the house. It's the one thing that I fought for in the divorce settlement. A house in the Hollywood Hills had always been my dream, and once I finally achieved it, I'd be damned if I'd just hand it over to him and his mistress.

The sprawling home, with its picturesque views and dark wood siding, is more reminiscent of Luke's log cabin than a typical Hollywood mansion. I fell in love with it the instant I stepped foot inside. The deep chocolate wood floors and river rock fireplace that kissed the twelve-foot ceiling had me signing on the dotted line before I'd even seen the entire house. Add in the view and nothing else could compare.

I stare out the bank of floor-to-ceiling windows lining the back of the house, overlooking the valley, and I can only think of one person. I'd asked him to come with me, and he begged me to stay. But in the end, neither of us got what we wanted.

I didn't have a choice. I had to come back. I'm not here for

Jeremy or because he asked me to return. Really, I'm not even here for myself. I'm only here for one person... Susan. She's treated me with more kindness than anyone in my own family ever has, and I can't turn my back on her now.

Luke didn't seem to understand. No matter how I tried to explain it, he never would. It's just another example of how different we are and why we wouldn't work, but when I'm with him, none of that matters. He makes everything else melt away. I've never been so present with someone. It probably had to do with the lack of distractions. No cell phones, television, or Internet makes focusing on each other inescapable.

I'm so lost in thought I don't even hear the front door open.

"Madison."

I jump and spin around to face Jeremy. My heart pounds furiously in my chest and I narrow my eyes. "What the fuck? You can't just let yourself in, Jeremy. This isn't your house anymore."

He waves me off with his usual cocky attitude. "I still have a key."

I roll my eyes, but I want to hurl myself across the living room and wrap my hands around his neck. "Gimme the key."

He strides forward, dangling the key between his fingers. "You'll have to earn it."

I square my shoulders, place my hands on my hips, and glare at him. "I've earned it by sucking your dick since we were teenagers, only to have you cheat on me."

He presses his hand to his chest and staggers backward like I hurt his feelings. "Ouch. You wound me with your words."

"Your acting doesn't work on me. Just give me the goddamn

key."

"It used to work." He smiles and runs his hand through his hair, giving me his signature headshot smile. "What happened?"

Folding my arms in front of my chest, my gaze turns icy cold. "The fairytale illusion of you has worn off, Jeremy. What are you doing here?"

He places the key on the mantle of the fireplace that splits the windows and the view. He slides his hand across the smooth mahogany mantle and pauses near the photo from our wedding. "We were happy then."

I take a step toward him and place my hand on his chest. "Jeremy." My voice is sweet, too sweet, but he's clueless.

He glances down at me with hope in his eyes. "Yeah?"

How can he even be serious? After all the shit he put me through, does he really think I want him?

"This..." I lean forward, almost pressing my lips to his.

"Yeah," he breathes, turning his head to line our mouths up perfectly.

"Will never happen," I say quickly and push against his chest, rocking him backward.

"Madison."

"What do you want?" I grab the key from the mantle and jam it in the back pocket of my jeans.

"I thought we could drive over to see my mom together."

"I don't need an escort."

Looking at him now, I can't remember why I ever loved him. He's always been self-absorbed. Everything was about him and his career. I thought I fit into his life and that I was a priority to him, but

I was just foolish.

"I'm not escorting you. Don't be difficult."

"Difficult?" My voice cracks.

How dare he call me that. During our entire relationship, I caved to his every whim and desire. When he couldn't make rent with his acting gigs, I worked double shifts bartending to make ends meet.

"Well, yeah. I'm trying to be a gentleman, and you're being a bitch."

"Get out." I'm surprisingly calm. I can't even muster enough emotion to yell. I'm not angry with him. I'm disappointed in myself for wasting years of my life in a relationship with a man who only loved one person—himself.

He balls his hands into tight fists at his side and his top lip curls before he speaks. "You think that asshole loves you?"

"It doesn't matter, Jeremy. You're not part of my life anymore. That's the one thing I do know for sure. You lost your place the day you slid between someone else's legs."

"You're fooling yourself, Madison. He's just using you for pussy. You mean nothing to him."

His words are meant to sting, but they don't. There's nothing Jeremy can say that would make me think that Luke doesn't have genuine feelings for me. Sure, we started out as a wild, uninhibited sexual escapade, but it's morphed into something more...something deeper.

"I obviously meant nothing to you either."

"You always lived in a dream world."

"Last time I'm going to ask. Go, Jeremy, or I'll tell Susan that you're treating me badly."

His stare hardens. "She's sick. You wouldn't dare."

"Wanna bet?" I cock my head and smirk, finding an inner strength that I never knew I had when dealing with him.

Weeks away have given me clarity. Spending time with Luke has given me a renewed sense of self and inner strength. There's nothing Jeremy can do to change that. I'm no longer the woman I was before, but he's still the same asshole. But I'm no longer looking at him through rose-colored glasses either.

He stalks toward the front door, mumbling to himself with his arms flailing around like a madman. "You always were a bad fuck," he says over his shoulder before walking out and slamming the door.

The old me would've cried from his declaration. I would've been wounded by his words, but I no longer believe anything he says. "Asshole," I mutter to myself, giving him the middle finger even though he can't see it.

An hour later I'm settling into a chair at Susan's bedside. She's a shell of the woman I once knew, hooked up to so many machines that I can't tell which cord goes with what contraption.

"Madison," she whispers behind the oxygen mask, reaching out to me.

I smile softly and take her hand in mine, placing it at her side. "Susan, I'm sorry I didn't come sooner."

My apology is genuine, but it doesn't seem to be enough. What do you say to someone who is dying? There aren't words to adequately describe how you feel about them when they're knocking on death's door. Susan has been a part of my life since I was a kid and knows exactly how I feel about her, yet I want to say more.

"How are you, my sweet girl?"

Tears sting my eyes. "I'm fine, Mom."

A faint smile forms on her lips, and she squeezes my hand tightly. "My son still being an asshole?"

"Jeremy is Jeremy. You know." I shrug it off, because no more explanation is necessary.

Susan knows exactly what kind of man her son is and everything that he did to ruin our marriage. He's the last person I want to talk about when this very well may be the last time I speak to her.

"Find your happiness." She shifts in her bed and grimaces.

"I am." I nod, causing the tears that lined my eyes to slide down my cheeks.

"Don't cry for me, love. I had an amazing life." She smiles softly and releases my hand. "Crawl up here with me."

I don't hesitate doing what she asks. Kicking off my shoes, I climb onto the bed, careful not to lie on any tubes, and settle into the crook of her arm. This is our goodbye. I know it's the last time I'll see her, but I can't quite believe it's true. I don't want to either.

She places her hand against my back and holds me as tightly as she probably can. "Most men aren't like Jeremy. I've had a blessed life with his father. I wouldn't trade a day of my time with him for someone or something else."

"I know you love Jim." I curl into her and close my eyes, memorizing her smell, feel, and sound. Even on her deathbed, Susan possesses the elegance and calmness that's always drawn me to her.

"Don't settle for anyone who won't put you first. You hear me?"

"I do." My fingers curl against her gown. I never want to let go.

My heart aches for her. For my loss. A life without Susan is something I'm not quite sure I can bear. She's always been a constant in my roller coaster life, especially during my separation and divorce from her son.

"I'm dying, Madison."

"I know," I whisper softly as more tears cascade down the side of my face, wetting her shirt.

"But I have no regrets about my life. I can't think of one thing I'd do differently. Instead, I'm surrounded by people I love and more happy memories than one should be allowed to have. I want the same for you. Find that happiness and don't let go."

I glance up at her. "No regrets. I promise."

"I love my son, but don't go back to him. He isn't worthy of you."

I blink slowly, letting her words sink in. She's spoken them before, but this time they have more meaning. She's spilling her soul to me and imparting wisdom before it's too late. "I love you," I tell her, but I want to repeat it over and over again until my voice is hoarse, but instead I cry harder.

"I love you too, Madison. You're the daughter I never had. Don't be sad for me. Be happy that I had such a blessed life. If you want to really remember me, find that slice of happiness and the one who makes you breathless when he's near."

"I love you," I say again, because all other words fail me.

We lie like that until she falls asleep, clutching me tightly to her body. I stay a few more minutes, watching her sleep, before I crawl off the bed and slip on my shoes.

"Goodbye, Mom," I whisper and bite down on my lip to stop the sob that's climbing up the back of my throat.

She looks so frail. I want to scoop her into my arms and make her feel the peacefulness she's always given me. I stare down at her for another minute. I take a mental picture of her and recount our conversation to store away when things get rough.

As I walk out the door, I turn one last time and mouth, "I love you," before running down the hallway of the hospice center and bursting into tears.

LUKE

I lasted four hours without Madison before the walls started closing in on me. I filled a bag with some clothes and headed out the door without a second thought. Nothing felt right without her there. I should've never let her go alone. The thought of LA and the people and traffic makes my skin crawl, but nothing compares to the ball of unease in the pit of my stomach without her by my side.

Before I hit the road, I stopped at the Avalon and asked Lou for directions to the address that Madison jotted down on the hotel stationary before she left. I try to make sense of his chicken scratch and focus on my destination instead of what's going on around me. I've never driven on busier roads than those in LA. My heart's racing but I keep my attention trained on where I'm going and not the incessant blaring of car horns around me.

My muscles relax when I finally pull off the highway and start winding through the Hollywood Hills. The homes I pass—at least the ones that aren't hidden by gates and fancy landscaping—can only be described as mansions. They're grotesque in size and opulence. There's no mistaking where I am. Northern California is no match for the overindulgence and sin of Hollywood.

I slow in front of Madison's home. It's smaller than I expect compared to the other homes in the neighborhood, but still overshadows the quaint cabin I've been living in. I'm surprised by the country feel of the dark brown home that blends in with the trees and brush around it.

I take three deep breaths, exhaling slowly after each one, and pull into her driveway. The sun sets in the distance, giving everything an ethereal glow. Her car is parked just outside the garage and the lights are on inside the house. I hoped she'd be here when I arrived, because I didn't want to wait outside too long. People around these parts probably aren't keen on strangers, especially ones who look like me.

The tightness is back as I walk to the door. Maybe she's pissed at me for not coming down with her, but I'm hoping my presence now makes up for it. I knock with two quick raps and square my shoulders, trying to be patient as I wait.

I scan my surroundings as a nosy neighbor snaps a photo of me over the bushes. People in Hollywood are strange, but I give him a quick wave so I don't seem unfriendly. The door swings open and the air in my lungs whooshes out as soon as my gaze lands on her gorgeous face.

She stares at me in disbelief. "Luke?"

Before I can speak, she hurls herself into my arms and buries her face in my neck. "Thank God," she whispers against my skin.

I lift her and let her legs wrap around my middle. "I couldn't be away from you," I admit, holding her tightly.

I missed the feel of her against me. I didn't think being apart, even for a few days, would be an issue until the silence set in sooner this time and I couldn't take another minute without her.

Her hands cradle my cheeks as she peppers my face with kisses.

"I was about to drive back up because I missed you so much." Her face has splotches of pink, and her eyes are swollen, but she smiles through her tears.

"You've been crying." Guilt floods me. I should've never let her come back here alone.

"I already saw Susan." Her head drops to my shoulder.

I carry her inside and kick the door closed with my heel, not willing to separate our bodies for a second. "How is she?" I don't take in the beauty of her home until I'm seated on the couch with her curled in my lap.

"She's as can be expected."

"How are you doing?" I glance down at her, trying not to get distracted by the amazing view outside the windows lining the back of her house. It's almost as beautiful as mine on my mountaintop. For being smack in the middle of Hollywood, there's more greenery than I expected, and it doesn't feel claustrophobic either.

"Awful," she says. "But better now that you're here."

Leaning back, I pull her with me, adjusting our position so we're both more comfortable. My body's already reacting to her nearness, her warmth, and the scent that's hers alone. "I'm here for as long as you need me."

She stares up at me wide-eyed with a smile and more tears. "Do you mean that?"

"I do," I tell her, and I mean every word. "I'll stay."

"I know this place isn't for you."

"A month ago, I wouldn't have said you were for me either." Touching my lips to hers, I close my eyes and relish in the feel of her against me.

She pulls away and laughs softly. "You've come a long way, Mr. Dawson."

"Only because of you, Ms. Atwood."

She settles against me and silence falls between us. But unlike when I'm alone, it's not deafening. It's comfortable and warm, just how everything with Madison always is. There will be a time to make love to her and a time to talk, but for right now, I just want to hold her.

My eyelids feel heavy and I fight to stay awake, but she drifts off first. Sleep hasn't been easy for me in years, but there's something about Madison that chases away my demons and puts my mind at ease. She's still in my lap, with her body slack against mine, as her soft snores pull me under too.

CHAPTER FIFTEEN

MADISON

I wake up just before noon in my bed, exactly where Luke had moved me after we'd crashed on the couch hours earlier. I'm rested, but my body aches from crying. I cried for Susan yesterday, but so many other things crept in as I let my emotions take me under. I mourned the death of my relationship with Jeremy, realizing that while he didn't have the same power to hurt me as he once did, coming to terms with the failure of us would probably occur in unexpected and painful waves.

And I grieved over Luke's absence, not quite knowing how we would work or if we could. I searched for answers, for the perfect scenario where we could keep being happy together, but the answers eluded me until he showed up at my door. Then I didn't need to search. I just needed him to hold me. Perfection was a night in his arms, no matter what the future might hold.

Yearning for his touch again, I roll over, but he's not there. Instead, a handwritten note rests on the pillow beside me.

Went for a drive. Be back soon. Love, Luke

I rise and go to the kitchen, spurred by the hope that he might be back already. He's an early riser, and I'd slept especially late. But the house is empty. I can sense its emptiness even before I check every room to be sure. I end my journey by the windows that look out to the valley. I may have loved that view more than I loved Jeremy toward the end. Being reunited with it gives me a sense of peace—peace that I had too little of when we'd shared this home.

I don't want to leave here, but I want Luke in my life too. I know he could never leave his quiet life for mine. I can't imagine how difficult the trip here must have been, yet he made it.

Tears burn behind my eyes again. Goddamn, I'm like a faucet that won't turn off.

Refusing to succumb to my emotions for another day, I force myself to clean up. I shower, get dressed, and eat breakfast. With nothing else to do, I go around the house, room by room, tidying and purging things that I no longer need. When I get to the living room, I notice the wedding picture is face down. Luke must have seen it. I cringe a little and take that as a sign. That particular memory belongs in the past, not on the mantle. I take it and put it into a box as the front door creaks open.

I recognize Luke's footsteps. Heavy and sure. My breath catches when he comes into view. He may not want to be here, but he owns the room everywhere he goes. Something's different about him though.

I light up with a smile when I place it. "You shaved!"

His lips quirk up a little. "Just this once. Don't get used to it."

I laugh and go to him. Finding that warm perfect place in his arms again, I breathe him in and sigh. "I missed you. Where were you?"

He gestures back to the entryway where several bags are sitting. "I got a few things so I could take you out tonight."

I pull back and give him a wide-eyed look. "Take me out?"

"I figured while I'm here I could take you out. Like on a real date or something. The lady at the hair salon suggested a few places that you might like."

"The salon?"

I can't hide my shock, and Luke laughs and smiles. I hadn't expected to see him so at ease here. I certainly hadn't expected him to venture into the city that sometimes I didn't even want to face.

Taking a closer look, I realize his hair looks different too. Still past his shoulders, but it looks healthier and is neatly trimmed at the ends. I'd been dying to take my conditioner to it for weeks, so I celebrate a small victory seeing these milestones met without me nagging.

"You did all this for me?"

He's silent a moment and leans in to touch his lips to mine. "Something like that," he says. His lips are warm and his skin is so smooth.

I revel in the new sensation as we kiss, but before I can get carried away, he takes a step back. "I want to do this right." He glances down at his watch. "We have a reservation at five thirty. With it being last minute, it was the only time I could get. Can you be ready in an hour?"

"Definitely. Where are we going?"

He smirks and turns away from me to go down the hall toward the bags. "It's a surprise. Go get ready."

L U K E

An hour later, I'm pacing the living room checking my watch. Madison takes for goddamn ever to get ready. Even with weeding through some new clothes and convincing myself to give up my boots tonight for some nice Italian leather shoes, I was ready in half the time. I hope she likes what she sees, because I feel like an imposter. I miss my cotton T-shirts already. Still, I managed to find quality clothes that are comfortable.

I hear the click of high heels on the wood floors and turn. Jesus, Mary, and Joseph.

I can see now how the natural beauty I fell in love with could easily pass for a celebrity on the arm of her ex. She's stunning in a shimmering red wrap dress that falls just past her knees. Her heels are shiny black with red soles and make her legs look a mile long. For the first time since I met her, she's wearing her hair up, though small tendrils are hanging loose around her face.

Her face. That's what really has my heart stopping. Her gaze is intense on me, her expression more serious than I want on a night like tonight.

"What's wrong, Maddy?"

She looks me over and blinks several times. "We can't leave the house."

"Why? Is everything okay?"

She exhales loudly and puts a hand on her hip. "Number one, women are going to be crawling all over you. Number two, it's suddenly become way more important for you to fuck me than for us to have dinner."

I laugh and go to her. "Knock it off."

She puts a hand on my chest when I go to hold her and she stares up at me. "I'm completely serious. You're totally irresistible right now. Who are you and where are you hiding my rugged mountain man?"

I warm at her compliment. It makes the hassle and stress of getting to this point all worth it. "He's not going anywhere, I promise. You can hold out this once. And no one's going to be crawling all over me when I've got you on my arm." I touch the tip of her nose because I'm afraid to screw up her makeup. "You look really pretty. Different, but pretty."

She blushes a little. "I am a makeup artist, you know."

"I know, but you don't need all this to be beautiful to me."

She smiles and cocks her head. "It's fun though. I'm grounded enough to know that clothes and lipstick and pretty shoes don't make me beautiful." Her smile fades a bit. "Does it bother you?"

"No. This is you. We're in your home, your town. We're doing things the way Madison would tonight. And for the record, you're stunning."

So stunning that I'm having a hard time keeping my hands off of her. We're already late so I usher her out the door and drive us to the restaurant in her car, letting her navigate the whole way. The sun is setting and the music in the car is playing low. People are driving like assholes, but having Madison with me is like having armor going into battle. I once told her that I loved the way she wanted to protect me, even if I didn't need it. But I'm wondering now if I was lying to myself, and to her. Maybe if I never left my cabin I wouldn't need protecting. But being part of the bigger world, being here with her,

I'm not sure if I could do it alone. At least not right away. Could I ever get used to this life?

A short while later, we're seated at a table for two at Culina. The patio and fresh air are especially nice. Gas heaters provide warmth and ambience. But we're far from alone, and seeing other people gawk at her already has me a little agitated. It's more evidence of why I can't let her go, not now, not ever.

Madison is radiant, unaware of just how entranced I am by her. A certain kind of energy rolls off her. I can't place it, but it's infectious.

"You look happy," I finally say.

She looks up from her menu with a smile. Her lips are full and red, and I want to taste them so badly.

"I am. This is perfect. It's been so long since I had a night out like this. You have no idea how nice this feels."

The waiter comes, interrupting our moment. I try not to be annoyed, because Madison is happy and I don't want anything to spoil that. She orders a martini and I order a beer because I don't know what the hell else to do. I close my menu and figure she should order for me too. I'm undeniably out of my element. Food is food.

We get our drinks, and when the waiter leaves us alone again, Madison leans back into her seat and brings the translucent red liquid to her lips. It's definitely more erotic than watching her drink coffee. I'm struggling to rationalize why we ever left the house now. Maybe she'd been right. I'm about to suggest we order to go when she sets her drink down and speaks up.

"So tell me, what's all this about? As happy as this makes me, I know it can't be especially comfortable for you."

I nod and worry the inside of my lip. There are so many things I want to tell her. Things that could upset her. Things that could give us a future. I'm not good at this, but I have to try.

"I realized something this morning while you were sleeping."

"What was that?"

"I wasn't sure what to do with myself, so I poked around the house a little. Sorry, but I'm kind of useless here. Probably how you feel at the cabin. No purpose. I get it. So I took it all in. The expensive house. The view. All your nice things. I saw pictures of you and him, and it hit me that you bought that place together and you've made a ton of memories there with him."

I tighten my jaw and her eyebrows come together.

"No, Luke. You can't think that way. It's my house now. I fought for it—"

I wave a hand to try to stop her. "Just hear me out, okay? I understand it's your home, and he's in the past. But for a few minutes there, I freaked out. I told myself I was stupid for coming. I was even more stupid for ever believing that we could find a way to be together."

Silence stretches between us, and she stares down at her lap. "I've had those same thoughts."

I nod, because I don't blame her one bit. We're in a difficult situation and the answers aren't always clear or easy.

"I was going to get my things and get out of your life for good, because clearly I have no place here. But then something hit me. Like a brick to the face. I thought about how uncomfortable I was in that moment, and I thought about how all that would go away when I was back home. Then...I realized that the place where I *was* comfortable wasn't really comfortable anymore when you weren't there. That's what got me out here to begin with. Something's changed. I've changed, and now I can't go back. I'm stuck in this middle ground with you, which is where we said we wanted to be. It's scary as hell, but you're home for me now."

Tears glimmer in her eyes, and I'm worried I've ruined everything.

"I feel the same way, Luke. I want to be with you. I can't express to you how much. But you...this..." She gestures between us. "I don't want you to feel like you have to change for me. I'll love you anyway."

"I know that. And I realize you took a chance on me. I don't know how many days you spent in my shitty little cabin without any of the comforts you were used to. But I figured, as long as I'm here, I can try to fit into your world more. I can't make any promises, but I'm trying. It's not all bad."

A smile tugs at her lips. "No?"

I take sip of my beer and sit back. "No. I'm going to make a mess of you later, but for right now, the view is damn fine from where I'm sitting."

A flush works its way to her cheeks, and I take that opportunity to look her over for the hundredth time. Her nipples are poking through the red fabric now, and it takes all my willpower not to reach across the table and mold my palms around the perfect curves of them. It's been forty-eight hours since we've had sex, and I'm ready to lose my mind. The hunger I have for her just won't wane.

The food arrives, and for the moment I'm grateful for the break in conversation, not to mention the sexual tension. My first confession went over pretty well. But there's more I have to tell her, and I'm scared to death she won't go for it.

My courage deserts me until we head back to her house. I can tell the martinis are making her frisky, because her hands keep straying to my groin. I catch them and kiss her fingertips, fully aware of how hard I'm getting and how she's effectively distracting me from the things I need to say.

The second I park, she leans over, and we're engulfed in a hungry kiss. I'm falling into the raging desire I feel for her—the desire to fuck and love and show her without words everything she means to me.

I place my palms on her cheeks and pull away enough to catch my breath. "I have to tell you something."

"What is it?"

I lean back in my seat and stare out the windshield. LA is a mass of city lights. In silence, I can see the allure. The glitz and the glamour is something else. I can only hope I mean more to her than this city does. I inhale a deep breath and begin.

"To anyone on the outside, it probably looks like I don't have much of anything. But the cabin isn't all I have."

She threads her fingers into mine. "I know. I Googled you."

I frown and look over to her. "You did?"

"After you kicked me out, I needed to know more about the mystery man who'd given me the best sex of my life."

"And..."

She shrugs. "And I saw your old Facebook account. I saw that you owned the land that the Avalon is on."

"I inherited it, but I own a lot more than that. That's what I wanted to talk to you about."

She leans her head against the seat and waits. She's so beautiful... so perfect. I look forward again, admiring the home that doesn't feel like it belongs here.

"I know you love this house," I say quietly.

"I love you more," she whispers.

I close my eyes, because I feel like my heart is going to beat straight out of my chest. Her admission gives me the courage to say more.

"Ever since I joined the military, I put everything I earned into buying land that I might want to live on or invest in later. I own several acres about an hour and a half north of here. It's a lot closer than Avalon, but it's nothing like the city."

I brave a look in her direction. She's chewing on her lower lip.

"What are you suggesting?"

I swallow hard and hold her gaze. "I'll move there. We could move there. I could build us a house you deserve. You'd be close enough to the city to work when you need to, and I won't have to deal with car horns and crowds all the time."

"What about this place?" She gestures to the perfectly good home she now owns.

"We'll stay here in the meantime. I'll make it work. Kills me to say it, but it'll probably be good for me. I'm not saying it'll be easy, but it's a step in the right direction."

Her breathing picks up, and I'm panicking on the inside.

"Madison, it's a beautiful spot. Right by a lake, mountain views. Trees everywhere. No neighbors in sight. I could be happy there, but only if you're with me. I need you with me."

She's quiet a long moment. I'm not sure what more I can say, how much more soul I can bare...

"Good God, say something."

She releases her lip. "Electricity?"

"Of course."

"Running water?"

I smile a little and the panic starts to ebb away. "Anything the city girl wants, except the city."

She leans forward again and sifts her fingers through my hair. "Sounds absolutely perfect."

MADISON

I'm reeling from Luke's offer. I'm overwhelmed in all the best ways. That Luke wants to make a life with me in the middle ground we promised to explore together. That he wants to build me a house with his bare hands. That he's come this far and is willing to go farther for the sake of us.

We leave the car and rush inside. Our hands are everywhere, and it's more than desire fueling my movements. I'm in love. So in love with this man I can barely breathe. He lifts me into his arms like I weigh nothing and carries me to the bedroom. He lowers me by the bed and unties the wrap that holds my dress in place. The fabric falls away and pools at my feet. For a long time, he simply stares. Seconds tick by and my skin warms unbearably. Need simmers through me until I'm ready to boil over.

"Luke, touch me."

He takes a step closer and slips his arms around my torso. "Tonight, I'm going to take you in ways I haven't yet."

I hold my breath and wait for him to elaborate.

He traces his fingertips lightly across my lips. "Mine." He trails them down to my nipple and pinches it. "Also mine."

I flinch, but the sensation he leaves is pleasant and adds to the fire raging inside of me.

He hooks his thumbs over the thin elastic of my panties and pushes them down. Still gazing into my eyes, he drags his touch through the folds of my pussy and then sinks a finger into my wet heat. "This is mine," he says, his voice low against my skin.

I close my eyes with a breathy sigh and bow into his touch. I lift my leg to hook it over his hip, trying to deepen the penetration. Instead of giving me more, he withdraws and uses my position to his advantage, teasing his fingertips over my anus. He breaches the opening before I can object—one finger and then two, lubricated by my own arousal.

My mouth falls open and a small cry escapes.

"This is mine, Madison. And I'm going to have it." His tone is full of love and determination and raw sexual need.

I can't resist him. Arguing is pointless, because he's right. I'm his. I belong to him, more than I've ever belonged to anyone.

I'm ready to build on that small miracle, because it feels so incredibly right. It feels like the next step of a life I worried had no course forward. If it starts with letting Luke push me past some of my sexual hang ups, then so be it.

He twists inside my untried flesh. I dig my fingernails into his broad shoulders at the unexpected pleasure that hits me.

"Take what's yours, Luke."

He kisses me fiercely and then releases me, urging me down to the bed. Instead of coming after me, he riffles through a nearby bag and returns with a bottle of lubricant and a small pink vibrator.

My eyes widen. "You bought those too?"

He smirks. "What do you think?"

"I had no idea how ambitious you could be." No wonder he was gone so long.

I expect him to move me how he wants, but instead he settles between my legs and hovers his lips over mine. Looking deeply into his eyes, I savor the warm press of his body against me. I savor all of it. His possessive yet patient touches. His kisses, deep and raw with emotion. He works me into a frenzy until I'm begging him to take me.

"I need you," I beg, lifting my hips against his, desperate for more contact.

He's maddeningly close, so hard and ready for me. When I think I can't take a second more of this torture, he turns me so I'm lying on my side and spoons behind me. Any anxiety I'd had before has left me. All I can think about is having him inside me.

Then he's there, slick and hard, pushing past the tight ring of muscle. The sensation is intense, almost taking my breath away. He moves his hips rhythmically, each time claiming me a little deeper, until my breath catches. Then he slows, kisses my neck, and nibbles my earlobe.

"You're perfect, Maddy," he murmurs against my ear.

The way we're coming together now reminds me of the first time, when I wasn't sure I could take all of him. In the same way, I let go. I surrender and I trust. I curl my fingers around his hand on my hip and push back into his next thrust.

"Fuck," he groans, pleasure thick in his voice.

He tightens his hold and the slow dance of our bodies joining picks up speed. I take him to the root and then he's powering into me.

I'm in disbelief...that he's so deep, that I've taken all of him, and even more, that I'm enjoying it.

I feel like I want to come, even if I have no idea how that's possible right now. Then he pushes the little vibrator into my hand and switches it on. With his hand covering mine, we trail the little toy over and around my clit.

"Come for me, baby. Let me feel you come."

He's breathless, and I love that I'm the one who has him that way.

He pounds into me, but his rhythm falters. He's close and so am I. I put the vibrator right where I need it and press hard.

Seconds later, I cry out and seize around his penetration. I'm flying, feeling everything, pulled down into the most incredible sensations.

And I'm his... Utterly owned.

CHAPTER SIXTEEN

MADISON

Luke parks the truck and turns to me, but I'm too caught up in the beauty that's right outside my window to pay him any attention. I clutch my chest, breathless and in awe of the majesty of this secluded hideaway. This is going to be ours. Soon there will be no more his and mine. The thought of that sends a shiver through my body and warms my insides.

"Do you like it?"

"It's...it's..."

I can't find the right words to describe what's in front of me. We're thousands of feet in the air, perched on the side of a tree-lined mountain with nothing but wilderness for miles.

"This is ours," Luke says.

I drag my gaze away from our mountain and finally turn to him. My eyes burn as tears form. I'm overwhelmed by his generosity and selflessness when it comes to us. "It's perfect."

He pulls my hand from my chest and nestles it between his palms. "Madison. I want to build our dream home on this spot. Just over there." He motions with his chin to a clearing near the southern edge. "I want nothing more than to make you happy."

I don't look because it doesn't matter where he builds the house. Luke will be there and that's the most important thing to me—not the location. He'll build it with his own two hands, and I know every inch of the house will be built with love.

"I'll be happy anywhere, Luke. As long as we're together." I swallow hard and push back the tears that are still threatening to spill over.

"Well, then let's just go back to my cabin." He smirks, knowing full well that it's way too primitive for me.

"No. No." I laugh softly and shake my head at his playfulness. It's a side to him I've come to crave. "I want this house."

His lips slide into an easy smile and he moves across the seat so that our legs are touching. Goosebumps break out across my skin when he nuzzles my hair. Putting his mouth next to my ear, he whispers, "I'm callin' in my wish."

The tiny hairs on the back of my neck stand at full attention as if fleeing whatever craziness he's about to drop on me. "I thought anal the other night was your payback." I have a feeling his idea isn't going to be something I'll love.

"Nah."

He closes his teeth around my earlobe, sucking lightly and tugging until I'm unable to think and my breathing grows ragged.

"We're going to camp here tonight, survivalist style."

My eyes that had fluttered close while his mouth made love to my earlobe snap open. "Um, no." I pull away. He's not going to use his sexual powers to fool me into sleeping under the stars, rolling around in the dirt.

"Come on, Mad. It'll be fun," he tells me in a voice that would make someone who knows him like I do actually believe his words.

I cross my arms over my chest and stare out the window again at the wilderness in front of me. There are no homes for at least five miles and no help if something should happen. "It's too dangerous."

His fingers touch my chin, bringing my gaze back to him. "Bullshit. I'll protect you. I'd never let anything happen to you."

"But there are bears and things out here."

His eyebrows lift. "And *things*?"

"Uh, yeah. You know...other animals."

He laughs, shimmying his body closer, he pins me against the truck's door. "There's nothing to be scared of, except for maybe me."

My hunger for him intensifies, erasing the fear of the wide open wilderness. "Okay," I say too easily. I can't take it back once it's out of my mouth.

He leans forward, pressing his lips to mine. With his fingers still resting against my chin, he steals my breath with the most devastating kiss. There's as much passion and longing in the way our lips move together as there was the very first time our lips met. Nothing has waned for me, only grown more intense over time.

My heart's pounding, reeling from the realization that we're sitting upon what's going to be our spot, the slice of heaven that he's sharing with me. I snake my arms around his neck, burrow my fingers in his hair, and melt into him.

He pulls away first, breaking the contact I could've stayed in forever. Well, at least through the night, safe inside the cabin of his truck.

"I want to stay in here all night," he says, his breathing hoarse and affected.

"We can do that."

"There are things we have to do before nightfall." His hand slides down my neck, cupping my breast before thumbing my nipple.

I sigh, completely compliant with his wishes.

"Once we're done, I want to make love to you under the stars."

I envision Luke pumping into me slowly, the grass tickling my skin and the stars twinkling above us like a million little flashlights creating shadows across our bodies. Then the slow movement of his hips as he grinds into me, warming us from the inside out.

He opens the door and climbs out while I'm still inside fantasizing about his body moving against mine. I hadn't noticed the camping gear he had stowed in the back when he loaded my luggage. This idea didn't just come to him. He planned it from the moment I agreed to go back to his cabin so he could pack up his life and head back to LA.

"There better be a tent in there." I join him near the rear of the truck and start to pull out duffle bags of what I assume are supplies and toss them to the ground.

"I may have lied a little." He grins sweetly, but there's a hint of mischief in his eyes. "We're not going to be survival camping."

"We're not?" My insides that had twisted at the thought of roughing it for a night begin to relax. Luke wouldn't do that to me, especially after I went easy on him when I trimmed his beard.

"No. I have all the supplies we need for a relaxing night under the stars, including a tent and cooking supplies."

I scan the truck bed, looking for some groceries, but I don't see anything. "Food?"

"We're going to forage and hunt. That much will be survival."

I gasp, horrified at the idea of killing an innocent creature. "I won't hunt, Luke."

His eyebrows furrow and his gaze darkens. "I need meat. Especially if I'm going to fuck your brains out later. We can't live off leaves."

"I refuse to kill an innocent creature," I tell him and stand my ground.

He rubs a hand down his face and groans. "You eat meat, Mad."

"Sometimes," I lie.

"It doesn't just show up on grocery store shelves. It has to die sometime."

"Fuck," I hiss and my stomach turns. "I can't."

He hoists the final bag from the back and throws it over his shoulder before grabbing the rest in his other hand. "Fine. We'll forage." The last word sounds bitter coming from his mouth, but it doesn't matter. I think it's a win.

"Good." I follow behind him, watching my step as we walk through thick brush toward the edge of the tree line. But then it dawns on me that maybe there isn't anything up here to eat besides leaves and twigs. What will we do then?

I sit on a rock after Luke orders me to do nothing but relax while he sets up our camp. Watching him closely, I take in the way he moves when he's comfortable and in his element. His relaxed demeanor is sexy, and the ease with which he sets up everything perfectly turns me on. It reminds me of when I peeked at him through the window above his bed after the first time we slept together. Something about his ruggedness makes everything inside me come to life.

When the sun hangs a little lower in the sky, almost kissing the edge of the mountain, Luke pulls his shirt over his head and tucks it in his back pocket. Leaning forward, I rest my elbow on my knee and my chin in my palm to admire the view. His muscles ripple, hardening and straining under his skin with each movement. I'm fascinated. Even though I've seen them a hundred times, it never gets old.

He's mine.

The knowledge of that fact makes this okay. When I'm with him, I feel untouchable, cocooned in an impenetrable force field of his love. Luke Dawson came into my life during a time when I least expected it and turned everything upside down.

He saved me. He says I saved him, but in all honesty, he brought me back to the woman I was always meant to be. No longer did I live in the shadows of the man at my side. I finally had the type of love that Susan told me to chase.

But it was the opposite. I ran. He chased. We both fell together.

LUKE

A coyote howls in the distance and she goes rigid underneath me. "I got you," I whisper in her ear, slowly sliding back into her with sure strokes.

Her legs tighten around me and her fingernails scorch my back. Then she tilts her hips, taking me deeper and relaxing under my touch.

There's nothing but stars twinkling above us in a cloudless night sky. The flames of the fire flicker, creating shadows across her face. My body aches for her. There's not a second of the day that I don't want to be joined with her in some way. A kiss. A hug. Or buried deep inside her. Since the day she barged into my cabin, I haven't had my fill.

I knead her ass, digging my fingertips into the soft flesh as I thrust into her. The strokes are long and drawn out, meant to touch every inch of her inside. I've never had the primal need to mark someone before, but Madison brings it out in me.

Even now, seated deep, I want to go further and lose myself inside her. Madison makes everything else disappear—the worry, the fear, and the regret of the things in my past. None of it matters when I'm with her. She chases away the demons that have haunted me for years.

I gaze down at her, memorizing this moment. "I love you."

She stares up at me with darkened, lust-filled eyes. "I love you too." The words warm my insides hotter than any fire.

She sinks her heels into my ass, holding my body against her. I'm a willing captive to her wordless command. She moves with me, grinding herself against me until she starts to tremble. She's close, and I'm right behind her. Her muscles go rigid as her breathing sputters. Needing more, I thrust into her quickly and pull out, swiveling my hips with each forward movement. She rides the waves of pleasure, her nails biting into my skin. The pain-pleasure mix is enough to send me over the edge. The spine-tingling orgasm leaves me gasping for air.

Her legs unfurrow. She goes slack underneath me, but her nails remain buried in my skin as she holds my body against her. We gaze at each other for a moment, and I think she's going to speak. Instead she lifts her head and kisses me, feeding me the air I so badly need.

"Thank you." She pulls back far enough to look into my eyes.

"For what?"

"For everything." She smiles, releasing her grip on my back.

"I should be thanking you." I roll to my side, taking her with me. "You saved me, Mad."

She places her head on my shoulder and studies me. "I was a shell of my former self, Luke, until I met you."

"We saved each other." I pull her body close, leaving no space between us.

"It's really beautiful up here." Her eyes move to the sky and to the stars reflecting against the darkness in her eyes. "I can't wait to spend every night with you in this place."

My lips find her forehead. "Me neither."

She's mine. It wasn't all just a dream. I never thought I'd find someone else to share my life with again. But fate had other plans. Actually my dick did. If it wasn't for the fact that her naked flesh and soft moans stopped me at the springs, I never would've met her. Instead of lying under the stars with her in my arms, I'd be alone in my cabin watching the fire crackle.

Exhausted from the day and spent from her orgasm, she drifts to sleep in my arms. For a moment I think about staying outside next to the fire, but it's not safe enough. The coyotes in the distance haven't quieted, and remain too close for comfort. Moving slowly, I place my arms under her body and climb to my feet. She doesn't wake as I carry her toward the tent just a few feet away and set her down on the sleeping bag. I adjust her body around mine to keep her warm through the night. I close my eyes, find the peace that only she gives me, and let the songs of the forest lull me into a deep sleep.

I wake abruptly to the sounds of screams. I sit straight up and look around me. Madison's gone, but the spot to my side is still warm. Without hesitation, I grab the knife I had stowed under my pillow and rush to my feet.

"Madison!"

Panic rises inside me as she shrieks louder. They're terror-filled screams, echoing through the valley below.

"Madison!" I yell again, trying to gauge my distance by the way her voice carries through the trees. Pushing aside the branches, not caring that I don't have any shoes on, I bolt through the forest toward her pleas. Then I see it. A coyote has her pinned with her back flush against a tree. It's growling, showing its teeth in aggression. Madison is frozen and naked.

"Stop yelling," I tell her when she screams my name, finally catching sight of me. "She's feeding off your fear."

She seals her mouth shut, her eyes wide and her chest heaving in fright. "She wants to feed off me," she says quickly, trying to burrow her body into the tree.

I step forward. The coyote turns and shows me her teeth, but I stop my advance. Based on the time of year, I know there's a good chance she's protecting cubs who are probably stowed somewhere nearby.

"It's okay, girl," I say, dropping my voice to a calm, even tone. "We won't hurt you."

"Are you fucking crazy? Kill it."

Now she wants me to murder something, and for what? Defending her territory? I ate berries and leaves tonight in the name of saving animals. I wasn't about to kill the coyote unless it was absolutely necessary. "She's afraid, Madison. She's defending her home and probably her babies. Stay calm and keep still."

"Well, I'm afraid too," she says in a sweet, gooey tone.

I lift the knife slightly, just in case the beast pounces on me.

"Hey, girl." I try to draw its attention away from Madison. When I step on a branch and it cracks, the animal turns to face me, her growl dropping deeper. "We won't hurt you," I tell it. Even though it can't understand my words, I do nothing to seem aggressive toward the coyote.

Slowly she backs away and her lips close around her teeth. She looks at Madison and then back to me. We're motionless. Frozen like statues, waiting for her to make the next move.

Madison's eyes are wide and unblinking, but her body sags after the coyote makes a high pitched noise like a dog and then jots away from us.

"Fuck," she hisses, leaning over and clutching her legs for support. "I thought she was going to eat me."

"Look."

I motion in the direction of the coyote and her two pups hidden behind the brush. They squeal out a howl as three sets of eyes watch us through the moonlit darkness.

"They're so cute," she says, her expression softening.

I hold my hand against her when she goes to move. "Wait for them to leave." I shake my head. "And you wanted me to kill her."

"I'm an idiot." She pouts her lips, but keeps her gaze pinned on the two pups. "I don't know if this wilderness gig is for me, Luke."

I smile at her honesty, but I know she can handle it. "Just don't traipse around here naked, alone, and reeking of sex when we move here and you'll be fine. What in God's name were you doing out here?"

"I had to pee."

I shake my head and laugh at her ballsiness. "Next time wake me up. Don't come out here alone. I almost had a heart attack."

"I almost got eaten, so we're even." She laughs softly. "Can we go now?"

The coyotes have vanished. I nod and hold my hand out to her, ready to have her back safely in my arms. "Do you want to head up to the cabin?"

She curls into me and walks tucked underneath my arm. "What about our stuff?"

"Leave it. I plan to spend plenty of time up here. I'll get it next time."

"We can stay if you want."

"I'll never fall back asleep. Let's go, and we'll crawl into my bed later."

"Sounds like heaven," she says, looking into my eyes when we make it back to the fire. "I had a great time tonight."

I wrap my hands around her biceps, stroking her skin with my thumbs. "Even with the coyote?"

"Even with the coyote, because I was with you." She places her head on my chest.

I kiss the top of her head and thank God she wasn't hurt. "Me too, even though you took ten years off my life the way you were screaming."

"Would you have killed the coyote for me?"

"I would've killed it before it had a chance to ever touch you,

Mad."

"That's hot, Luke."

"What?"

"You were kind of badass back there. It's almost sexier than the bar fight."

"Fuck." I shake my head and pull away from her just enough so I can see her face. "Promise me that you won't do any more shit like that?"

She pulls her bottom lip between her teeth and bites down before a broad grin breaks free. "I promise."

The woman keeps me on my toes. I thought I had a pretty full life. I thought I was happy before she walked into my cabin uninvited. But I was wrong. I just glided through the days without any real purpose. Loving Madison has become the sole reason for my existence.

"Um, where are our clothes?" she asks, breaking my train of thought.

I glance around, but see nothing. "Somewhere around here."

"We can drive naked." She laughs. "I've never done that before."

We're a couple hundred miles from the cabin, but there's a good chance at this time of night that not another soul will be on the road. Sitting next to her, watching her tits jiggle as we drive down the dirt roads makes the risk of getting arrested entirely worth it.

"I'm game if you are," I tell her as we walk toward the truck.

"Life's short, Luke. Live a little." She nudges me in the ribs with her elbow. "You need to take a leap sometimes without overthinking everything."

I pull her into my arms and kiss her deeply. She doesn't realize it, but I leapt a long time ago, right into her arms.

EPILOGUE

MADISON

The new-car smell permeating the Land Rover is my only consolation during the bumper-to-bumper traffic that is keeping me from Luke. After hours of slow progress, the congestion leading out of the city finally breaks up. Thank God, because I'm ready to collapse the minute I get to my destination.

I'd been going non-stop with gigs all week and had spent the better part of the day dealing with high-maintenance models and stressed-out clothing designers for a fashion shoot. I can't lie. I thrive on the high. The hustle and the rush. The personalities and the drama. Los Angeles got under my skin a long time ago—the energy of the place and the promise of dreams coming true every day.

But when the time came to take a break, I ran in the opposite direction. North, to be exact.

Construction on our dream home had been underway for months. Luke couldn't stand life in the city, so he broke his vow and hired a few helping hands to speed up the process. I wasn't a purist when it came to home construction, so I didn't argue. I was looking forward to waking up every morning in our home on the mountain as much as he was.

Today, instead of driving down to my house in the hills, Luke insisted that I drive up and check out the progress. The night is black by the time I arrive on the property. Only my headlights guide my slow journey down the dirt path from the paved road to the house location. I put the Rover in park and let my jaw hang a little. The log wood frame along the top of the house is lined with hundreds of sparkling Christmas lights, and past the huge windows I spy a tree shimmering with lights and ornaments.

I grab my overnight bag and hurry toward the house, up the wide wooden steps leading to the hand-carved door, and over the threshold into the warmth of our home.

Our home.

I still can't believe it when I say it or even think the words. One glance around and I still can't lift my jaw. I haven't been here in weeks, and I'm in disbelief how much has been accomplished. Wide-board pine floors have been installed and stained a light grey, adding to their rustic feel. Light fixtures are in place, and the walls even have the colors I'd chosen months ago.

A fire roars in the massive fireplace framed with river rock—a project that Luke had taken on himself, inspired by the fireplace I'd be leaving behind at the old house. I slip off my coat and let it fall to the floor. The grand room is empty, save the tree that must stand fifteen feet tall in front of the window, and a worn leather chair. I bite my lip and go to the chair, trailing my fingertips over the warm, cracked armrest.

Memories flood me with that simple touch. I'd spent my first night in Luke's cabin nestled in this chair. I'd trimmed his beard for the first time straddling his massive naked body in this chair. Luke and I had fucked in this chair more times than I could count, but like most of his simple possessions at the cabin, it had stayed behind.

"I hope you don't mind."

I lift my gaze toward Luke's deep voice. He's leaning against the archway that leads into the kitchen, his hands tucked into his worn blue jeans and his legs crossed at the ankle. My breath catches. I haven't figured out how not to be awed by his beauty yet.

His beard has grown back, but he keeps it tidy for me. His hair has grown a couple inches and falls in amber waves past his shoulders. His eyes... Those clear blue depths hold me captive. He comes closer, pressing the air out of my lungs with each step. I only breathe when he leans down and presses a soft kiss to my lips. Contact...relief...an overwhelming and reassuring rush of his love.

"I wasn't sure you'd love me moving my shitty old furniture into your brand new house."

I laugh softly. "Well, this is *our* brand new house, and you know as well as I do, this chair has some serious sentimental value."

"I can't argue with that." He smirks and laces his fingers into mine. "Thanks for coming up. I would have driven down to get you, but I wanted to finish a few things here."

I scan the room again, no less in awe of his progress. "It looks amazing. I had no idea it'd come this far."

His smile broadens and I catch a hint of mischief in his eyes. "I have a lot to show you. Are you hungry?"

I shake my head. "I had a protein bar before I left work. I could really use a glass of wine though."

He leads me to the kitchen, which holds more surprises.

Granite, faucets, and, yes, running water. I clap my hands in glee, even though I'm certain these modern conveniences mean almost nothing to my better half. Still, he seems pleased that I'm so happy. The way he strives for my happiness is something I'm working to get used to also.

He pours me some wine and gives me a tour of the rest of the house. We end in the bedroom. Instead of an empty, dark room like the others, I'm greeted with a warmly lit and fully furnished room. In the center is a king size bed made out of thick logs. Similar in style but much bigger than the one that had graced Luke's cabin on the mountain.

"I made it myself." Luke's chest puffs out with pride.

I chuckle. "I love it. And I have a feeling it'll get plenty of action."

He nods and drops his hand firmly atop one of the bed posts. "With that in mind, I made sure its construction would stand up to rigorous use."

I giggle and lean into his warm muscular chest. He circles his arm around me, and I lift my chin so I can look up into his eyes. He leans down, but a short, high-pitched sound outside stops him before our lips can touch.

I frown and look out to the clear double doors that lead out to the balcony from the master bedroom. "What was that?"

Luke purses his lips and leaves my side. "I'll check it out."

I stay put, because I'm still not completely comfortable with the wildlife factor. After my run-in with a protective momma coyote months ago, I have learned that the best way to respect the wild outdoors is to stay primarily indoors.

Luke disappears through the slider and into the darkness.

I wrap my arms around myself when the cool night air whips in. I consider going to the door when a flash of white fur whizzes in. I scream loudly and launch myself onto the safe high ground of our bed, glancing around wide-eyed for whatever the hell it is.

"Come here, girl." Luke's voice is light. He's on his haunches, his gaze riveted on some invisible point under the bed. He makes kissing sounds and holds his hands out, palms up. "That's my girl. Come to Daddy."

A second later, the little puff of white fur appears past the edge of the bed. It's a puppy, wagging its tail so enthusiastically that it can scarcely walk in a straight line toward Luke.

Laughter bubbles up from my stomach, inspired by relief, and also the realization that a tiny innocent puppy just scared the living shit out of me. I sink to my knees, drop my face in my hands, and start to giggle.

Luke closes the door, shutting out the cold, and brings me his new friend. Carefully, I take the small bundle from his massive hands. The tips of her little pointed ears and wet nose are black. She is all fur and almost no mass.

"She's a Malamute," he says.

She looks like a little wolf pup. I hold her close to my chest to soothe her and kiss her furry head as she wiggles excitedly. Without a doubt, I'm quickly falling in love with the little creature.

"She's so precious. What's her name?"

He shrugs. "I figured you could name her whatever you want. She's here to protect you and watch over you when you're scared and I'm not here." He pauses and runs a finger along her collar. "But I was thinking maybe Susie."

I look up and blink when emotion stings my eyes. Susan's passing earlier in the year had hit me hard, but I knew deep down that she was still with me, urging me toward the happiness she so wanted for me.

"It's up to you. If you wanted something different, I can get her a different collar," Luke says softly, his voice wavering a bit.

I shake my head and look down adoringly at little fuzz ball Susie. "It's perfect. I love it. I love her." I push her fur aside to take a closer look at her collar. "Susie" is embroidered in silver thread on the back of the band, and a metal tag clinks at the front. I finger the metal tag for a split second before I notice the enormous diamond ring that hangs against it.

"Luke." My voice is barely a whisper.

I'm trembling, shaking my head in disbelief.

Gently, Luke takes Susie from me and unhooks the ring from her collar. He goes from standing to down on one knee, as I stare down in shock and awe from my kneeling position on the bed. Holding the ring in one hand, he takes my hand in his other.

I'm riveted on him, singularly focused on this moment. Luke and nothing else. He draws in a deep breath before speaking.

"You've had me on my knees from day one, Madison. I love it here, and I love you. I want to worship you, protect you, and love you every day for the rest of this beautiful life we're building together. I want to wake up every morning to you in my arms. I want to explore the hell out of the middle ground and push each other outside of each other's comfort zones, together. And one day, I hope I can talk you into giving me some beautiful children who are just as amazing as you are. But right now, all I want is to know that you'll be my wife.

Madison, will you marry me?"

Tears glimmer in his eyes, and I have to stifle back a sob that wants to rip free.

"Yes, of course. Yes, yes."

I wave my shaking hands toward the ring that must have cost him a fortune. For being a simple man, he'd really gone all out. The second he slips it onto my finger, I launch into his arms.

He lifts me off the bed, and I wrap my arms and legs around him. We hold each other so tightly I can hardly breathe, but I don't care. I've never loved him more. We kiss, a passionate, all-consuming kiss that goes on forever. I'm not sure we'll ever stop, but then the sound of Susie's tiny footfalls prancing around us distracts me. I smile against Luke's lips. I know, now more than ever, I've found my happiness in this man, and I'm never letting him go...

MORE MISADVENTURES

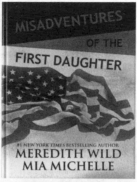

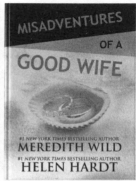

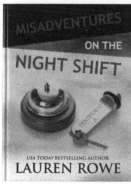

VISIT MISADVENTURES.COM
FOR MORE INFORMATION!

ABOUT MEREDITH WILD

Meredith Wild is a #1 *New York Times, USA Today*, and international bestselling author of romance. Living on Florida's Gulf Coast with her husband and three children, she refers to herself as a techie, whiskey-appreciator, and hopeless romantic. When she isn't living in the fantasy world of her characters, she can usually be found at facebook.com/WildMeredith. Additional information can be found on her website.

VISIT HER AT MEREDITHWILD.COM!

ABOUT CHELLE BLISS

Chelle Bliss is the *USA Today* bestselling author of the *Men of Inked* and *ALFA P.I.* series. She hails from the Midwest but currently lives near the beach even though she hates sand. She's a full-time writer, time-waster extraordinaire, social media addict, coffee fiend, and ex-high school history teacher. She loves spending time with her two cats, alpha boyfriend, and chatting with readers. Chelle can be found at facebook.com/authorchellebliss1. Additional information can be found on her website.

VISIT HER AT CHELLEBLISS.COM!